Tate couldn't stop reaching out and to his, couldn't help himself from wanting to step a little closer, to wrap his arms around her.

Duty was only part of it, he realized. He was attracted to Sabrina Jones...if that was even her real name. He didn't want to lose her.

She stared up at him, warring emotions on her face, until finally she nodded. "Okay, I'll stay. Just promise me that you're all going to be careful. If this guy turns his focus on you and Sitka and you can't find him, I want you to be honest with me. I want you to tell me so I can make my own decision about whether to stay or go."

He nodded, not breaking eye contact. "I promise."

But he knew it wasn't a promise he could keep. This wasn't a fight he was letting her take on alone anymore.

One way or another, they were going to end this here.

Acknowledgments

Huge thanks to the team at Harlequin, who has helped me bring fifteen books to readers! This book is better for the beta read by Caroline Heiter and the online #batsignal writing sessions with Tyler Anne Snell, Regan Black, Janie Crouch, Louise Dawn and Nichole Severn.

K-9 HIDEOUT

ELIZABETH HEITER

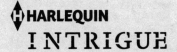

I love writing strong heroines. This book is dedicated to a few of
the strong women in my life: my mom, my aunt Andy, my sisters
Kathryn and Caroline, and my sister-in-law, Lamia.

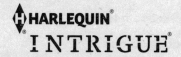

HARLEQUIN®
INTRIGUE®

Recycling programs
for this product may
not exist in your area.

ISBN-13: 978-1-335-55519-9

K-9 Hideout

Copyright © 2021 by Elizabeth Heiter

For questions and comments about the quality of this book,
please contact us at CustomerService@Harlequin.com.

Harlequin Enterprises ULC
22 Adelaide St. West, 40th Floor
Toronto, Ontario M5H 4E3, Canada
www.Harlequin.com

Printed in U.S.A.

Elizabeth Heiter likes her suspense to feature strong heroines, chilling villains, psychological twists and a little romance. Her research has taken her into the minds of serial killers, through murder investigations and onto the FBI Academy's shooting range. Elizabeth graduated from the University of Michigan with a degree in English literature. She's a member of International Thriller Writers and Romance Writers of America. Visit Elizabeth at www.elizabethheiter.com.

Visit the Author Profile page at Harlequin.com.

CAST OF CHARACTERS

Sabrina Jones—She's been on the run from a dangerous stalker for two years and she finally feels safe in Desparre. When her stalker finds her, she decides to make a stand, but it may cost her her life—or Tate's.

Tate Emory—The police K-9 handler is determined to help Sabrina end her nightmare. He never suspects his own past could threaten them both.

Sitka—The Alaskan malamute went from shelter dog to police K-9. Her tracking skills may be the key to finding Sabrina's stalker.

Brice Griffith—The new police chief supports Tate's decision to help Sabrina, but he's in the dark about Tate's secret past.

Dylan Westwood—Two years ago, Sabrina's boyfriend was killed by her stalker and Sabrina has been running ever since.

Jim Bellow—The Boston police officer went to jail for taking payoffs and trying to kill Tate—but Tate believes he didn't act alone.

Chapter One

Desparre, Alaska, was so far off the grid, it wasn't even listed on most maps. But after two years of running and hiding, Desparre made Sabrina Jones feel safe again.

She didn't know quite when it had happened, but slowly, the ever-present anxiety in her chest had eased. The need to relentlessly scan her surroundings every morning when she woke, every time she left the house, had faded, too. She didn't remember exactly when the nightmares had stopped, but it had been over a month since she'd jerked upright in the middle of the night, sweating and certain someone was about to kill her like they'd killed Dylan.

Sabrina walked to the back of the tiny cabin she'd rented six months ago, one more hiding place in a series of endless, out-of-the-way spots. Except this one felt different.

Opening the sliding-glass door, she stepped outside onto the raised deck and immediately shivered. Even in July, Desparre rarely reached above seventy degrees. In the mornings, it was closer to fifty. But it didn't matter. Not when she could stand here and listen to the birds chirping in the distance and breathe in the crisp, fresh air so different from the exhaust-filled city air she'd inhaled most of her life.

The thick woods behind her cabin seemed to stretch forever, and the isolation had given her the kind of peace none of the other small towns she'd found over the years could match. No one lived within a mile of her in any direction. The unpaved driveway leading up to the cabin was long, the cabin itself well hidden in the woods unless you knew it was there. It was several miles from downtown, and she heard cars passing by periodically, but she rarely saw them.

Here, finally, it felt like she was really alone, no possibility of anyone watching her from a distance, plotting and planning.

After a year and a half of living in run-down motels and fearing each morning as much as she feared putting her head on her pillow at night, she'd desperately needed a change. She hadn't expected to end up here. She'd driven north for days, finally stopping because heavy snowfall had made traveling farther impossible. And for the past six months, she'd stayed. There was something magical about Desparre.

It was far from the kind of place anyone who'd known her as a sun-loving city girl would have expected her to end up. Far from anywhere she would have expected to ever call home.

But damn, did she love it. If she had to spend the rest of her life in solitude, this was where she wanted to do it.

Tipping her head back, she closed her eyes

and let the crisp, cool Alaskan air refresh her. With a smile, she pulled out her phone to check the time. Although she had nowhere to be, she wanted to run into town early, then get back to do some work.

As soon as she saw the date on her phone display, her smile dropped under the force of her shock. Today marked exactly two years since she'd left New York City. Two years since she'd left behind everything and everyone she knew. Two years of missed birthdays and holidays. Two years of not being able to talk to her mother or her brother, not being able to see her friends.

A familiar ache welled up, one that only Alaska had been able to keep somewhat at bay.

When she'd said goodbye to New York, she'd expected—hoped—to be home long before now. The police couldn't guarantee they could protect her, but they were hunting for her stalker. She'd believed it was only a matter of time. But with her in hiding, new leads had probably dried up fast.

An image of her mom and her brother back in New York City looking at the calendar together popped into her mind. Her mom would be frowning, a tightness to her jaw that Sabrina had seen in her childhood. Her brother would try to comfort her, try to hide his own anxiety. But they would both be wondering where Sabrina was, wondering if she was okay. Wondering if she was still alive.

She tried to suppress the instant mix of anger and sadness. She'd explained to her family what the PI she'd hired had told her: disappearing was the only way to ensure her safety—and theirs. She wouldn't be able to contact them, and she couldn't tell them where she was going.

They'd fought her on it, but it hadn't mattered. She wasn't going to let anyone else die because of her.

Tucking her phone back into the pocket of her pajama pants, Sabrina stared into the woods, hoping to regain the peace she'd felt only moments ago. But tears pricked her eyes, and today even the woods couldn't ease the tension between her shoulders.

Six months was longer than she'd stayed in one location since she'd gone into hiding. Three months ago, she'd actually started venturing out for more than just essentials. This tiny little town had given her back something she hadn't felt in a long time. Something she hadn't felt since that very first contact from her stalker.

Despite all the solitude, she felt less alone than she had in almost two years.

She'd actually made friends here. Sure, they didn't know her real last name, and in her normal life, she would have called this level of familiarity simple acquaintances. But with two years of loneliness, two years of running whenever she saw a shadow out of place, it felt like real progress. It almost felt like a real life again.

Guilt surged at the very idea that she could just move on with her life, in any small way. Now, the three months of memories she'd built with Dylan felt so distant, so short. She'd been naive to invite him into her life with a stalker following her, leaving her his twisted version of love notes. It wasn't that she hadn't been taking the threat seriously; it was just that she'd thought the threat was only against her.

But on a brilliantly bright Saturday afternoon when she'd gone to meet Dylan's family for the first time at their lake house, Dylan had been late. She'd been annoyed until police had shown up to tell his family why.

He had died simply because he'd dated her. It was something she'd carried with her ever since.

Before Dylan was killed, police had been taking the letters seriously, but compared to the other crimes they were investigating, it was low priority. When Dylan had been shot inside his own home and then the letter arrived, telling her not to be sad because Dylan had been standing in the way of her true happiness, the police response had been much more intense.

A month later, though, they'd been at her door, their discouraged, too-serious expressions telling her everything she needed to know. With fingerprints and some DNA left behind at the scene of the crime, they were sure they'd get Dylan's killer eventually. But he wasn't in the system, so they couldn't match the forensic evidence to a name. In the meantime, he'd continued to contact her, somehow slipping past the cameras police had installed, and once, slipping a note into her purse on her way home from work.

Dylan's murder showed that her stalker was escalating, police had told her. She was in real danger, quite possibly his next target. They were committed to keeping her safe, committed to stopping the person who'd killed the man she had only just begun to call her boyfriend.

But they couldn't provide twenty-four-hour protection. And she hadn't been willing to risk anyone else she loved.

Sighing, Sabrina stepped back inside, all the healing powers of the Alaskan wilderness no longer working. The PI who'd helped her create a fake name and then disappear had set up a system, a place for her to check safely for updates. The investigator would post a specific message on her website if the stalker was ever caught.

In two years, there had been no updates. But no one else had been hurt because of her, either. If she had to spend the rest of her life running, at least she'd finally found somewhere she could imagine having even a fraction of the life she'd left behind.

If the years in between had taught her anything, it was that living like this could break your will, break your heart if you let it. Her stalker had taken the life she'd built, but he wasn't going to steal all of her happiness.

"Buck up, Sabrina," she told herself, then squared her shoulders to face the day. By the time she'd gotten dressed and was headed for the door, ready to run into town for some groceries, she felt almost normal. She was even smiling at the thought of trading small talk with the owner, Talise, who'd lived in Alaska all of her seventy years and always had good stories.

Then she opened the door, and the whole world spun in front of her. All the oxygen seemed to disappear as she gripped the doorframe to keep herself upright.

There was a single white card on her doorstep. On it, the same angled, spidery font she'd come to dread back in New York. The same bright red ink that reminded her of blood even more since Dylan's death.

The message was simple, exactly what she would have expected if she hadn't started to believe she'd finally outrun her stalker.

I've missed you.

Chapter Two

Her first instinct was to run. As far as she could, as fast as she could. Just like she'd done countless times over the past two years.

Instead, she put on latex gloves and picked up the card carefully by the corner, even though she knew it was wiped clean. Her stalker had left prints and a small amount of DNA at the scene of Dylan's murder but never on her notes. She sealed it in a plastic bag and then ran to her truck, almost tripping as she glanced around for any sign of him—a man she'd never seen but who'd somehow tracked her almost four thousand miles.

Then she was driving, white-knuckled, eyes dangerously focused on her rearview mirror, toward downtown Desparre. The roads were unpaved, and the rough winters didn't do them any favors. The rusted old truck she'd gotten at a steal when she'd crossed into Alaska six months ago jolted her with every uneven patch of road. Her head started to throb from her clenched jaw, shooting pain up the side of her head with each bump. But she couldn't seem to unclench it.

No one was behind her.

Of course, she'd been assuming that for six months. And yet, somehow, her stalker had found her.

Tears of frustration welled up, and she blinked

away the moisture, refusing to give him more power over her than he already had. If he could find her here—a place that felt like the end of the earth—was anywhere truly safe? Was running the wrong move?

It was time to find out.

As she steered her truck down the incline onto Main Street, right into the center of what passed as a downtown in Desparre, she ignored the cheerful laughter coming from the little park. A few months ago, a bomb had gone off in that park, shattering her illusion that Desparre was one of the most peaceful places she'd ever lived.

But people here were resilient, and they'd rebuilt the gazebo that had been destroyed. The scorched earth was now covered with green grass and blue irises, and the metal butterfly benches she'd admired when she'd first driven into town but had been blown to bits in the blast had been replaced with new ones. Residents who thrived through dangerously cold winters, who knew how to avoid the avalanches that could slide off the side of the mountain, had flocked back to the park as if the bombing had never happened.

She needed some of that Desparre resilience right now.

Parking the truck, Sabrina took a deep breath and glanced around the small downtown, looking for anyone who seemed unusually fixated on her.

The downtown was tiny, with a post office,

clothing store, bar, drugstore, grocery store and church lining the unpaved street. To someone who'd grown up in the big city, it looked like one of those fake towns where tourists came to see reenactments of miners showing off their pans of gold.

None of the people walking around, soaking in the sun as if it were ninety degrees instead of fifty-five, showed any interest in her. From three months of coming into town, she recognized many of them as longtime residents.

That was the thing about Desparre. It wasn't New York City. It was much bigger in terms of land size, but population density was minuscule in comparison. Yes, people came here to hide, many of them running from their own tragedies or threats. Some even running from the law. But most of them had lived here a long time. Most of them knew each other. They might wholeheartedly embrace a *Live and let live* attitude where they allowed everyone to keep their secrets— something she'd greatly appreciated when she arrived—but they still recognized the outsiders.

Maybe, just maybe, they could do what the New York City cops had been unable to accomplish. Identify her stalker and end her nightmare for good.

Glancing around one last time, Sabrina strode up to the other building located downtown, the police station.

Nerves churned in her stomach as she pulled open the door, wondering if she was being watched even now. Wondering if involving the police again would make her stalker more violent.

The front of the station was a small area mostly taken up by a desk where a young officer sat. His reddish-blond hair looked vaguely familiar, and she remembered he was the officer who'd been hurt in the bomb blast. Maybe he was still healing and had pulled desk duty in the meantime.

He looked up when she walked in, his expression a mix of boredom and friendliness. "Can I help you?"

"Y-yes," she stuttered, trying not to lose her nerve. "I-I'm being stalked." She held up the bagged note as he stood, his brow furrowed.

Then the door opened behind her, and a white-and-black dog bounded toward her.

"Sitka, sit."

The commanding voice, underlain with humor, made Sabrina's gaze jump from the dog up to the man coming in behind her. Nerves immediately followed.

Officer Tate Emory. She'd seen him around town over the past six months and been immediately drawn to him. She'd even talked to him a few times. Back in her old life, the six-foot-tall man in the police uniform with the angular cheekbones and the dark, serious eyes would have had her flirting hard. Here, she'd stammered her

way through their brief conversations, her gaze
mostly on the floor, hoping she'd be unmemo-
rable.

That was what her stalker had reduced her to.
Hoping no one noticed her. Hoping she could
slip through life silently, until what? He finally
caught up to her and killed her and no one even
knew to look for her body?

Shaking off the morose thought, Sabrina
glanced at the dog she'd never seen before, who
had followed instructions to sit—right at her feet.

Tate shook his head at the dog. "She's still a
puppy. She finished her K-9 training, but sometimes she needs to be reminded about her man-
ners."

At the words, Sitka glanced back at her owner
and wagged her tail.

Tate's smile at his dog faded as his gaze locked
on the paper Sabrina was still holding up. Then,
his attention was entirely focused on her. "Is
someone harassing you?"

She nodded, then blurted, "Stalking. For two
years." She almost succeeded in keeping her
voice steady as she added, "He's found me again."

Tate walked past her, using a key card to open
the door marked *Police Only*.

"I've got this, Nate," he told the other officer.

Then he looked at her again, his gaze project-
ing confidence. "Come on back with me, Sabrina.
Let's talk through what's going on, okay? We

take care of each other here. We'll take care of you, too."

As she followed him, Sitka sticking close to her side, something fluttered in her chest, something that felt suspiciously like hope.

THIS WAS *NOT* how he'd hoped to strike up a conversation with Sabrina Jones.

Tate Emory had seen her around town for the past half year, usually on the outskirts of Desparre. But to his frustration, it was always when he was in uniform, on the job. He'd struck up a few short-lived conversations with her, but he kept hoping to run into her when he was off duty. He'd wanted to get to know her a little more, maybe even ask her out.

Right now, though, seeing the fear in her green eyes, he just wanted to help. Holding open the door to the back of the station, he ushered her through.

His newly certified K-9 police dog, Sitka, followed. She was seventy-five pounds of Alaskan Malamute, a funny mix of puppy energy and police-dog intensity. He'd been petitioning the department—and his previous chief—for a K-9 practically since the day he'd joined the force five and a half years ago. The last thing Chief Hernandez had done before leaving Desparre was grant approval.

Now, after two months of training, his shelter-dog adoptee was a full-fledged police dog. He smiled down at her as she stayed in Sabrina's footsteps like the woman's protection detail.

"This way," he told Sabrina, leading her through the mostly empty bullpen toward the glass-encased office at the back where the chief worked.

When he knocked on the door, the new police chief, Brice Griffith, called out, "Come on in."

Chief Griffith was seven years older than Tate's thirty-one, with fourteen years of experience in police work back in Vancouver. He'd made the jump to Alaska with his young daughter in tow when the town's old chief had decided to follow her new boyfriend to Anchorage and return to detective work.

So far, Chief Griffith seemed like a fair boss. He was personable enough, though like most of the people in this town, he'd definitely come to Desparre to outrun something.

Not that Tate could throw stones. If the chief knew Tate's true history, he'd probably be fired on the spot.

"What's up?" Chief Griffith asked, standing as Sabrina followed Tate into the room.

"This is Sabrina Jones," Tate said, noting the surprise on her face that he remembered her full name. "She's being targeted by a stalker."

The chief frowned. "Take a seat," he told Sabrina, then added to Tate, "Close the door."

Tate did as he was told, then sat in the chair next to Sabrina. Sitka settled in the space between them, her ears perked as she glanced from Sabrina to Tate.

"This was left on my doorstep today," Sabrina said, handing the note to the chief.

The chief read it, then stared at Sabrina. "This isn't the first time you've been contacted by this person, I take it?"

"No. He followed me from New York." She took a shaky, visible breath. "I've been running for two years. I thought I'd lost him here."

Two years? Tate stared at her, wondering how he hadn't realized sooner she was trying to escape a threat.

He should have. Every time he'd spoken to her, she'd directed most of her responses to her feet. He'd thought she was shy, maybe even nervous because the attraction he felt for her was reciprocated. But the truth was that she'd been afraid of anyone taking too great an interest in her.

Had he gotten so comfortable here that he'd forgotten what it had been like in the beginning? Gotten to accept this life so much that he'd completely let his old one go?

The idea made an old ache start up in his chest.

Even though his previous chief had known his history, had helped him come on board with his faked background and fake last name, he'd spent a long time thinking he'd made a mistake. That staying in police work would be a way for the people who'd tried to kill him once to find him again.

He should have recognized that same fear in Sabrina, should have found a way to help her sooner. Some police officer he was.

Chief Griffith's eyes narrowed at him like he could see Tate's internal struggle, like he suspected Tate wasn't quite who he said he was. Then his attention was fully on Sabrina. "Tell us about this stalker."

She shifted forward in her seat, her hands gripping the arms of her chair as her wavy, blond hair fell over her shoulder, obscuring part of her face. "It started two and a half years ago. I began getting notes on my doorstep." She nodded in the direction of the note the chief had placed on his desk. "They all looked like that, with the red text and the creepy messages. The first one just said *I've been watching you.* They were always short, usually things like *One day, we'll be together* or *You must know how much I love you.*"

She shuddered a little, glancing at Tate and then back at the chief. "The first one spooked me, and my friends convinced me to call the police. Initially, they took my report but didn't seem that interested. But when this guy kept writing, they said they could officially call it a stalking case. Still, it didn't feel like much was happening until—"

Her head tilted toward her lap, her hair falling over her face even more until Tate couldn't see her expression at all. "I started dating someone."

Dread sank to his gut, suspecting where this was going before she continued. "Three months later, he was shot in his home. Then my stalker left me a note saying *Don't be sad. He was just in our way.*"

"That's when you ran," the chief said, sympathy in his voice and an expression on his face that told Tate he was familiar with that kind of pain.

The expression was gone too fast for Tate to figure out what it meant. Next to him, Sabrina swiped at her face quickly, like she hoped no one would notice.

Her head lifted again, and she squared her shoulders, nodding. "Yes. I hired a PI to help me disappear. I spent a year and a half running from one tiny town to the next, trying to stay below the radar. I never got another note, but sometimes I'd just start feeling…jumpy. So, I'd go somewhere else, get a different car, leave anything unimportant behind. Then I arrived here."

A smile trembled on her lips. "I've been in Desparre for six months. I've felt more normal than I had in a long time. I thought… I really thought I'd finally escaped. Then I got this letter. I considered running, but…" Her knuckles whitened around the edges of the chair, her jaw clenching. She turned toward Tate, pleading and hope in her gaze. "I want this to end."

The new chief had been here for a few months. Most of that time, Tate had been doing K-9 training with Sitka. But he'd still felt constantly on edge, worrying Chief Griffith would notice something off in his doctored personnel file and realize Tate wasn't who he said he was. He'd feared that the life he'd built for himself here could be destroyed at any moment. He'd worried about a threat to his life, too, but he was a trained police officer. He was armed and relatively dangerous if provoked.

What must it feel like to be a civilian with no training? What must it feel like to be completely alone, being chased by a threat that hadn't even been fully identified?

Not waiting for the chief's assessment, Tate said, "Desparre isn't New York. We have resources we can put on this."

He kept his gaze fully on Sabrina, wanting her to see in his expression how committed he was to helping her, but from the corner of his eye he could see the chief's raised eyebrows. Still, Chief Griffith didn't contradict him.

The fear in Sabrina's eyes started to shift, turning into tentative hope.

"We're going to find this guy," Tate promised. "It's time to stop running and let us make a stand for you. We're going to get you your life back."

Chapter Three

Sabrina Jones had chosen a good place to hide.

Desparre was a big town in terms of geography. It stretched from wooded patches with houses hidden among the trees through small commercial areas and across half a mountain. Besides the tiny downtown, they had other, more out-of-the-way spots to get supplies if you really wanted to stay unseen.

Tate had grown up on the other side of Alaska, in a coastal town that was much bigger and busier than Desparre but still boasted that wide-open-spaces Alaskan charm. But he'd lived in Boston for so many years that when he'd moved to Desparre, the expansive spaces without people had felt as foreign as the big city had initially seemed.

Still, he'd never hidden away in the woods or up in the mountains, like so many people did who came here running from something. He'd been confident in the backstory that had been created for him, confident that Alaska was too far for anyone to even think about searching for him. But the threat against him was one of revenge, not an obsessed wannabe-lover.

The fact that Sabrina's stalker hadn't given up after two years, hadn't found someone else to fixate on, was worrisome. His department back in Boston had handled a couple of stalker cases. They'd tried but been unable to keep either of those stalkers locked up, and he'd felt frustrated for the targets who'd continued to live in fear.

Tate frowned as he opened the back of his modified police SUV for Sitka to jump in. The department didn't have the money for a true K-9 vehicle; they'd barely been able to cover his and Sitka's K-9 training.

But all he'd really needed was the official approval. He'd been happy to shell out the money for Sitka's special stab-and bulletproof vest, happy to pay out of pocket for her vet bills and food. She was his partner, but she was also his pet. Every night after their shift was over, she came home with him. If all went as planned, eight years from now, she'd retire and just be his dog.

His puppy's tail wagged as she leaped into the vehicle. She knew it meant they were going to work.

He glanced back at her as he climbed into the driver's seat. "How about we practice your tracking today?"

Her tail thumped harder, and she gave an enthusiastic *woof!*

Grinning, Tate put his SUV in gear. But his smile faded fast as he thought about the message Sabrina had found. Being such a small town, they used the state's forensic lab for big, complicated jobs, but all of the local officers knew how to do basic work, like dusting for fingerprints. The note left on Sabrina's doorstep had none.

Maybe her stalker had left something else behind, like his scent.

Heading out of downtown, Tate turned onto one of the dirt roads that passed as a highway around here. Sabrina's address wasn't in the most remote part of Desparre, but she'd definitely picked a spot where people weren't likely to know she lived there unless she told them. Or unless someone spotted her elsewhere and followed her home.

Once they did that, the location was much less appealing. It was too far for neighbors to hear a cry for help, too secluded for anyone else to see a threat.

Gripping the wheel tighter, Tate wondered if they were doing enough. Based on what Sabrina had said about the investigation back home, there wasn't much to go on there, especially since NYPD had determined it was someone on the very outskirts of her life. Still, she'd been cagey with the details, flat out refusing to give them her boyfriend's name or the names of the investigating detectives back in New York. She'd asked them not to contact the police department there, insisting that her family's safety would be compromised if they learned where she was.

She'd looked so panicked that they'd finally agreed. The fact was that if the NYPD had gone two and a half years without being able to identify her stalker, even after he became a murderer, the leads in New York were slim. For now, it made more sense to concentrate on new arrivals to Desparre, people who might have tracked Sabrina here. After Sabrina had left the station looking a lot more confident and hopeful than when she'd walked in, he and the chief had finished mapping out a plan to keep her safe. They'd already given her an emergency-alert button that connected directly to the station. They had scheduled police drive-bys of her house multiple times a day, with scattered times to prevent her stalker from seeing a pattern. Sabrina was supposed to call them if she had the slightest concern, wanted a police escort somewhere or just wanted someone to do a walk-through of her home.

Hopefully, they'd spot the guy before he could get close again. But Tate and the chief had agreed they needed to get more proactive rather than just hoping her stalker made a mistake.

So today, he and Sitka would get a chance to test out their training.

As he pulled into Sabrina's long dirt driveway, Tate glanced around. There wasn't much to see besides trees. Someone passing by on the street wouldn't spot the cabin without binoculars or very keen eyesight. To drop the note on the doorstep, her stalker had probably left his vehicle on the road and crept through the trees. Otherwise, Sabrina could have seen him coming.

When Tate put the SUV in Park, the curtain moved on the front window, and Sabrina's face appeared in the crack. He hopped out of his vehicle and waved at her, then let Sitka out, too.

Sabrina stepped outside, scanning the woods before her gaze settled on him.

"Sitka and I are going to try a little tracking work," he told her.

She looked surprised, probably having expected he was doing a check-in. Her gaze went to Sitka, whose tail wagged at the attention.

"She's a tracker dog?"

"Actually, she's a dual-purpose dog." He rubbed her head, the thick coat perfect for Alaska, even if Malamutes weren't usually used as police dogs. "She specializes in both patrol and tracking."

"Patrol?" Sabrina smiled, humor in her eyes that had been missing every other time they'd spoken. "Does she write speeding tickets with those big paws?"

Tate smiled back at her, wishing he'd realized something was wrong one of the dozens of times he'd chatted her up around town and reached out to her sooner. "Close. She's my partner. So, if I need to chase someone down, she can help me. Or she can clear a building or provide security. She's trained to bark and detain, too. That's pretty much exactly what it sounds like. She finds someone and keeps them from running so I can come in and cuff them."

"Can I pet her, or is that off-limits when she's on duty?"

"Go ahead." Although he didn't let civilians pet Sitka while she was actively tracking or doing a specific patrol task, she was great with people. Letting the people in Desparre pet her also made them comfortable having her on the force, something which was brand-new for the town.

She was off leash now because they weren't downtown, but at the chief's request, Tate had been using a leash in town while people got used to her. He hoped she'd bring good press and pave the way for expanding their K-9 team in the future.

Sabrina smiled at Sitka as she rubbed the dog's ears.

Sitka's head tilted up like she was enjoying the attention, and her tail thumped.

When he'd gone to the shelter, he'd been hoping to find a young German Shepherd or Malinois, both typical breeds for police work. But as soon as the little Alaskan Malamute had seen him, she'd dropped her chest to the ground, backside still in the air, tail wagging, and barked. She'd wanted to play. And he'd been totally charmed.

The shelter hadn't known anything about her background, other than that she was obviously a Malamute and not afraid of people. She'd been found alongside a highway, way too thin but anxious to please.

Although he'd been approved to become a K-9 officer back in Boston before the attempt on his life, he'd never actually gotten a dog or gone through training. He'd done research on traits that made good police dogs, but ultimately he'd known that whether or not Sitka would make a good partner would only be determined once they started training.

Still, his mind had been made up the moment she'd demanded his attention. He had to take her home.

After some initial hurdles with her energy level and distractibility, she'd received high scores in all of her certifications. But now was the real test.

She'd only been patrolling with him for a few weeks, not enough time in a place as low in crime as Desparre to really test out her skills. And so far, there'd been no reason for her to do any tracking in real conditions.

Tate could happily stand around half the day, chatting with Sabrina while she pet Sitka, but he was on duty. "You can watch from inside if you want. We're just going to see if Sitka picks anything up here."

The smile that had stayed on her face the whole time she pet Sitka faded, replaced by wariness at the reminder of her stalker. "Okay. Thank you."

Tate watched her walk inside, heard the loud

click of the dead bolt turning and then said to Sitka, "Let's see where this guy came from."

Most likely, they wouldn't get much. But knowing which side of the street the stalker had parked on might indicate whether he'd come from the direction of town or somewhere more secluded. Tate was betting on the latter, betting that her stalker had chosen an out-of-the-way cabin, too.

Directing Sitka onto Sabrina's porch, he told his dog, "Scent, Sitka!"

She sniffed the air briefly, then her nose went to the ground, and she barked at Sabrina's door.

"Another one. Scent again," he told her, knowing she'd just alerted on Sabrina, since the woman had been on the porch most recently. Hopefully, the stalker's scent was still here, too.

If it was, Sitka should be able to find and follow it. Compared to the paltry five million scent receptors in the noses of humans, dogs had two hundred and twenty-five million.

Sitka's nose went back in the air, then down to the ground, sniffing around for a minute. Then she walked off the porch, nose still down. She headed straight into the woods off the side of Sabrina's porch like he'd expected. But instead of bounding toward the street, she ran around the side of the house.

Had the stalker crept around Sabrina's home, maybe peered in her windows? The idea made his fists clench, but it shouldn't have surprised him.

Instead of circling the cabin, Sitka raced into the woods, away from Sabrina's house.

Frowning, Tate ran after Sitka. He glanced back once, saw the big sliding-glass door at the back of the cabin, Sabrina's face peering out at them.

Then he was hurrying after Sitka again. She was definitely tracking a scent. Her nose came up a few times, as she slowed and sniffed the air, before dropping down again.

As they moved away, the woods got more dense. It wasn't long before he glanced back, and even knowing where the cabin was, he couldn't see it.

He couldn't imagine a stalker finding a random road somewhere else alongside these woods and then trekking through the trees for miles to leave a note on Sabrina's doorstep. But Sitka seemed certain, her tail wagging as she ran, because K-9s were trained to think of their police tasks like games. She kept a pace that was hard to match.

Then a noise up ahead put Tate on instant alert. A rustling, like someone was there. Had the stalker stuck around this long?

His hand dropped to the grip of his gun in his duty belt even as he continued to scan the woods ahead of Sitka.

She'd slowed, the fur on her back rising. The fact that she hadn't shifted slightly and raced toward the noise meant it wasn't the same person who'd left the scent she was tracking.

Tate swore as a shape materialized from behind the tree. A black, furry shape, a solid twenty pounds lighter than Sitka, followed by another.

His pulse spiked, and he tried to keep the panic out of his voice as he called, "Sitka, come! Back up, girl."

She backed toward him, her movements slow and controlled, like she was backing away from a suspect so he could take over.

Only this time, she was backing away from a pair of baby bears. The question was, where was the mom?

Then there was more rustling, and Tate saw her. A cinnamon-colored black bear lumbering after her cubs. Her head swiveled in his direction, then Sitka's, as her babies continued to run perpendicular to his dog.

"Sitka, slow, girl," Tate said softly, hoping the bear wouldn't see either of them as a threat. The bear might have weighed about the same as he did and was probably only a foot shorter if she stood, but he was no match for her strength-to-weight ratio. And his pistol was no match for a furious mom protecting her cubs.

Sitka's movements became even slower, but she kept backing toward him, showing no fear even as the bear got up on her hind legs, still watching them.

Then the bear dropped back down, and Tate held his breath, wishing he'd brought the bear horn he kept in the back of his vehicle. He reached for his pepper spray with one hand and got ready to shout and try to seem as large as possible if she rushed them.

He let the breath out slowly as she followed her cubs instead, but his pulse didn't return to normal until she was out of sight and Sitka had backed up against him.

"Good girl," he whispered, stroking her head as her tail wagged.

She looked up at him, then back in the direction she'd been tracking, ready to keep working.

But Tate didn't want to risk running into the bear again. They usually weren't dangerous if you were smart, but he didn't want to startle a mom with cubs. He had no idea how far these woods went before they led to a road. "We'll look at some maps instead," he told Sitka.

Her talents were unproven in the real world, and Tate knew his boss would question whether the stalker had actually trekked so far through the woods, not giving himself easy access to a getaway vehicle if Sabrina or someone else had spotted him. But Tate trusted Sitka.

He glanced around, seeing nothing but woods in all directions. If Sabrina's stalker was confident enough to sneak up on her house through a mile or more of woods, he was more skilled than a typical city boy. Or maybe he hadn't just recently found Sabrina. Maybe he'd been right behind her all along and only today decided to make himself known.

But if he'd been in Alaska for six months like Sabrina, what had changed to make him announce himself? And what did that mean for Sabrina's safety?

Chapter Four

"He came through the woods."

Sabrina stared at Tate, a sick feeling in her stomach. "Through the woods?" Had her stalker seen her in the mornings when she stood outside on her deck, enjoying nature, sometimes in her pajamas? How close had he gotten without her ever suspecting anyone was there?

She resisted the urge to reach up and touch the alert button that was hanging on a thin chain around her neck. There was comfort in knowing Tate and the rest of the Desparre PD were on the other side of it.

"Yeah, I know it's strange," Tate said, misinterpreting her surprise. "I'm not sure where he came from, because we ran into a bear."

"A *bear*?" She glanced from him to Sitka, relieved that they both looked fine, then realized she'd basically been parroting his words since he'd returned to the house after trying to track her stalker.

Flushing, she stepped back a little and did something she hadn't done in two years. "You want to come in?"

The words felt foreign on her lips, and she realized just how much had been stolen from her. Even the little things, like feeling comfortable enough to trust anyone in her home, had become a thing of her past.

Not anymore. She stared at Tate, watching a debate play on his face. He was on duty. But he wanted to come inside.

She hadn't been imagining that the attraction she'd felt in the brief moments they'd spoken over the past six months was reciprocated. A zing of excitement darted through her, lodging in her chest and quickening her breathing.

"Can you tell me more about the tracking?" she asked, hoping it would make his decision easier if it was connected to his work.

"Sure." He wiped his boots on the mat, and Sabrina held in a smile.

She wouldn't have cared if he'd brought in all the mud in the forest. Despite the nerves suddenly dancing in her stomach, this was the most normal she'd felt in a long time.

"Come on inside, Sitka," she told his dog, and the Alaskan Malamute glanced at her owner.

When Tate nodded, Sitka bounded inside, danced a circle in the tiny entryway and then sat.

Laughing, Sabrina asked, "How come I've never met Sitka before?"

Tate stepped inside, closing the door behind him and throwing the dead bolt for her.

The loud sound made her jerk, her nerves doubling at having a man she'd admired from afar for six months crowding her entryway. He was tall and lean, but whether it was the six inches of height he had on her, the fact that there was obvious power in his frame despite his lack of bulky muscle or just his nearness, the space suddenly felt much smaller.

"I only got Sitka a few months ago," Tate answered, either not noticing or pretending not to see her discomfort. "The two of us have mostly been down in Fairbanks for the past two months getting our training."

No wonder she'd seen him so infrequently lately, even though she'd gone to town more often, hoping to run into him.

"What was that like?" she asked, tilting her head back so she could see his face better.

"A lot of work." He grinned, and the expression softened the sharp lines of his face, made him seem even more approachable.

It eased her nerves but only increased her awareness of how little space was between them.

For six months, every time she'd seen this man, she'd wished she dared risk asking him out. Now he was in her home.

Taking a step back, she gestured for him to follow, then headed into her combined kitchen and living area. The big sliding-glass door, nestled between two equally large windows, showcased a gorgeous view into the forest. This had always been her favorite spot in the house. But now, as she peered into the dense woods, she wondered if the solitude that had always made her feel so safe and alone had just been camouflage. She wondered how often someone else had been staring back at her unseen.

"He's not out there now," Tate said.

When she glanced at him, there was sympathy on his face, and anger, too, like he was as upset about the invasion of her privacy as she was. "If he was, Sitka would have found him?"

At the mention of her name, the dog hurried over to stand between her and Tate, tail wagging.

Tate reached out and stroked Sitka's head. "Yes. The guy trekked a long way to get here."

"I wish *he'd* run into the bear," Sabrina muttered, earning a brief laugh from Tate. Then, she awkwardly gestured to the couch facing the view. "Have a seat. Do you want something to drink or—"

"No, I'm fine." Tate settled on one side of the couch, giving her plenty of space. Sitka followed, lying beside the sofa.

Sabrina sat on the opposite end of the couch, twisting slightly to face him. He looked at ease in her home, and she wondered if being a police officer brought that level of calm confidence or it was just his natural personality.

She was the opposite, usually filled with a jittery energy, a need to be active or creative. Sitting still had always been a challenge. As she stared at him, he watched her quietly, and she wondered if he could tell that she wanted to jump right back up and move. She wondered if he could tell just how much nervous excitement filled her at his nearness.

"How does it work, the tracking?" she blurted, partly because she was curious and partly to fill the silence.

"Whenever you move, you leave a scent behind. So, on your porch, Sitka actually scented on you first. She followed the scent to your front door." He laughed, then continued. "Then she found the second scent, presumably the stalker. She sniffs the air to locate a scent and then puts her nose to the ground. Dogs can track scents for long distances, through water, through all kinds of weather conditions. It's pretty amazing, actually."

Sabrina looked at the Alaskan Malamute, who had enough of a gangly puppy look that she couldn't have yet been quite full-grown. "Very impressive."

As if she knew she'd just been complimented, Sitka's tail wagged.

"Did you grow up with dogs? Is that why you wanted to be a K-9 officer?"

"I *didn't* grow up with dogs, which is probably why I wanted to be one," Tate said, leaning back against her couch, shifting to more fully face her.

Suddenly, despite his uniform, despite the reason he was here, it felt more like a first date than

an update on the investigation. Not just that, but
it felt like a *good* first date, the kind that would
ultimately lead to a second date.

"I always wanted a dog. When I saw Sitka in the
shelter, she was just so—" he grinned at her, his expression full of affection "—energetic and goofy."

Her tail wagged again, and he added, "She was
also smart and eager to please, which helped her
in training."

Then Tate's expression got more serious.
"What about you? Did you have a dog? Who's
waiting for you back home?"

"I didn't have any pets, mostly because I lived
in a fifth-floor walk-up in New York City. But
I guess it was a good thing, since running with
a pet would have been harder and might have
been a way to track me. I'm close to my mom
and brother, though. They're both back in New
York. I haven't dared to contact either one, and I
miss them every day. The PI who helped me said
it was safer to cut all contact on my end unless
there was an emergency."

Tate frowned slightly, sympathy on his face,
but instead of turning it into a discussion about
her stalker like she'd feared he might, he said, "I
haven't seen my family in a while, either. I can
imagine how much you must miss yours."

She nodded, trying not to dwell on the memory
of the last time she'd seen them both, when they'd
fought her so hard on her decision to go into hid-

ing. Now, after all the sacrifices she'd made, her stalker was still right behind her.

Shaking off the frustration, she focused on the fact that she had Tate here. After two years of trying to keep everyone at a certain distance, she deserved at least one normal conversation. One semi-*truthful* conversation. She hadn't told him her real last name to protect her family's safety, but this was the closest she'd felt to normal in more than two years. She could actually be herself and not have to watch every word, worrying she might accidentally let something slip about who she really was, why she was here.

And talking to Tate was easy, comfortable. Despite her hyperawareness of him, she'd gladly just sit and chat with him all day.

"Have you always lived in Desparre?"

He looked surprised by the conversation turn. "No. But my mom's family is part Tlingit, and they've been in Alaska forever. My dad's family has a long-running charter business, so they've been here a long time, too. My parents divorced when I was young, and I was an only child, so I was shuttled back and forth a lot. We lived in a bigger town than this, but it was still small enough to run into one parent while I was with the other. They get along okay now, but in those early years, not so much."

"Where in Alaska did you grow up? I got here and pretty much headed straight north until I was snowed in. But I've heard some parts of Alaska actually get a real summer." She grinned, because the locals always seemed silently amused by anyone who wasn't native to Desparre and was bundled up when the locals were wearing shorts.

"I..." Tate frowned, shook his head slightly. "My family is from here originally, but I actually grew up in the Midwest. I moved to Desparre five and a half years ago."

She stared at him, wondering why his words were suddenly so stiff, his gaze averted like he wasn't giving her the full story. But why would he lie about where he'd grown up?

She'd probably just become unpracticed at getting-to-know-you conversations. But if she was truly going to stop running, if the Desparre PD was going to help her make a stand here, then maybe all the things she thought she'd never have again were actually possible. That meant she needed to figure out how to talk to a man like Tate Emory again.

After what had happened to Dylan, she'd vowed never to date again, never to put anyone else in danger. But now, staring at Tate, seeing how dedicated he was to helping her, seeing her interest reflected back in his gaze, everything seemed possible again.

WHAT HAD HE been thinking?

Tate had managed to spend five and a half

years without telling anyone—not even his old partner, Peter—the real details of his past. Half an hour with Sabrina at her house yesterday, and the words had just come out of his mouth, without him even realizing his mistake until she'd asked which Alaskan city he'd lived in as a child.

Hopefully, his awkward attempt at correcting his mistake hadn't been an obvious lie.

Tate had spent most of his morning patrol going over the conversation in his mind, trying to figure out if he'd just blown his own cover. He didn't think so. Despite having been on the run for two years, Sabrina seemed to take his word at face value. It made him feel worse about needing to lie to her.

No wonder he hadn't entered into many deep friendships, let alone any relationships, since he'd come here. It wasn't in his nature to lie to people.

He missed having someone who knew the truth about him. Even though he and Chief Hernandez had rarely talked about his real past, knowing that someone here was aware of his secret had made him feel less alone.

It had also given him a stronger sense of security. Chief Keara Hernandez had let him go through the police academy as if he really was a rookie, then brought him onto the force. She could face legal repercussions if the truth ever came out, but she'd done it as a favor to an old family friend who worked for Witness Protection. That family friend also knew Tate's family. The man had agreed to help him hide outside official channels. That favor had allowed Tate to return to a career he loved, let him return to a state he loved.

Yes, he was more than a thousand miles from his childhood home, from his family. But the beauty he'd taken for granted as a kid made him feel closer to them now, even if he couldn't see them. It made him feel one step closer to who he really was.

Chief Griffith had no idea he wasn't actually Tate Emory, security guard from the Midwest who'd moved to Desparre for a change of pace and a chance to fulfill a lifelong dream of becoming an officer. Tate had no idea what the new chief would do if he found out.

As he parked his SUV outside the police station, ready to spend some time in downtown after a morning patrolling the outskirts, Tate vowed not to be so careless again. He wasn't sure what about Sabrina Jones made him so unguarded, but he needed to be especially vigilant around her. Just because she was being honest about her past didn't mean he could do the same.

As if thinking about her had made her appear, Tate spotted Sabrina walking out of the grocery store. She had one small bag in her hand and was glancing around anxiously.

"Come on, Sitka." He hopped out of the vehicle and put on her leash. "Let's go say hello."

Woof!

His dog's enthusiastic reply caught Sabrina's attention. As soon as she met his gaze, her shoulders relaxed, and she smiled. It was a real smile, not the nervous, hesitant kind she'd given him over the past few months. A smile born of the belief that she knew him, that she could trust him.

It made guilt bubble up, and Tate tried to suppress it. She might not really know him, but she *could* trust him.

He headed toward her, and she met him halfway, immediately bending to pet Sitka. "How has your day been?" She peered up at him from where she'd crouched down. "Did Sitka help you write a lot of speeding tickets today?"

He grinned back at her. "Nah. She was in a good mood. She just handed out warnings."

Woof! Sitka's tail thumped, and she glanced back and forth between them, as if she knew she was the subject of conversation.

"What about you? How are you doing?"

When Sabrina stood again, she was smiling, too, looking far less worried than when he'd spotted her. "I'm just trying to live my life like normal." She shrugged. "Well, as normal as it gets these days." She lowered her voice, glancing around again, even though the closest person was across the street. "I don't suppose you've made any progress at figuring out who's doing this?"

Tate shook his head, expecting disappointment, but she didn't seem surprised. After two years of running, her expectations were probably pretty low. "Just keep being careful. The chief and I talked through strategy yesterday after you left the station. I know you're worried about us contacting New York, but we'd like to dig into your history to see if fresh eyes make anything pop."

She immediately tensed. "My cousin's wife works at the station. You contact them and she'll find out and it will get back to my mom and my brother. Then they'll come here. And after what happened before…"

Tate held up his hands, understanding her fear for her family. "Okay. Most likely, we'll find him by looking at people here. So, if anything seems unusual or anyone gives you a weird feeling, let us know. There's nothing too small for us to check out."

She gave him another smile, but this one was shaky. "Thanks."

"Why don't you drop your groceries in your car and walk with me and Sitka? We were going to the park, to let some more people meet her."

"Okay."

There was happiness in her voice, and as he walked with her to her rusted old truck, he tried not to let it ignite a similar thrill in him. She was a citizen who needed his help. Yes, he'd been considering asking her out for months—something he hadn't done any of since he'd gone into hiding himself—but things had changed. He couldn't be distracted by her, not when he needed to be thinking about her safety.

Still, he couldn't keep his gaze from lingering on the way the sunshine created golden highlights in her hair, the way it emphasized the smoothness of her ivory skin. Couldn't keep his mind from traveling down an imaginary road where she wasn't living in fear and he didn't have to keep his real identity a secret.

She dropped off the groceries, and then they headed toward the park, Sitka tugging slightly on the leash and giving him glances as if to ask *Why am I wearing this?* In that moment, it felt like he was off duty. It felt like he was just enjoying the company of a woman he liked and a dog who'd given him family here.

From across the street, Yura Begay gave him a nod. The gruff former Marine and lifelong Alaskan resident owned a check-cashing place on the outskirts of Desparre. He was known to be rude, but ever since Tate had gotten Sitka, he'd been warming up. Tate hoped it was a sign of how the rest of the town would respond.

It was the middle of the day, and the sun felt fantastic after the brutal winter, but it had been raining half an hour ago, so there were only a handful of people besides Yura downtown. Still, there were a group of kids in the park, parents chatting on the benches nearby. Hopefully it would give Sitka a chance to charm some more people and Sabrina a chance to relax. One thing he could be relatively confident in: if her stalker had tracked her across the country over the past two years, he was pretty unlikely to be chasing her with a wife and kid in tow.

The closer they got to the park, the slower Sabrina's steps became.

"Do you know anyone here?" Maybe he could introduce her to some of them while he was introducing them to Sitka.

She shrugged. "Some. I've been trying to talk to people more, but it feels insincere when all the typical questions you ask someone you've just met are things I have to lie about."

The same guilt filled him, the desire to share his secret with her, to trust someone enough to be truly honest. But it was a selfish wish, one that could put her in danger. So, he kept quiet and just continued walking.

As they reached the park, Sitka whined, tugging on her leash like she wanted to cross the street.

Tate frowned, pulling her back as he glanced around, trying to figure out what had caught her attention. He didn't see anything. Then again, despite two months of intense training, Sitka was still a year-old puppy. And walking with Sabrina probably felt more like off duty to Sitka, as well.

"Come on, Sitka. You'll like talking to the kids."

She glanced at him, whined and tugged once more, then gave in.

As he stepped onto the grass, a shout from the far side of the park commanded his attention.

"He's going to fall! Help! Help!"

The group of parents who'd been talking and laughing near the benches jumped up as one and raced toward the gazebo, where a boy of about seven had somehow managed to get on the roof. Now he was dangling off it.

"Stay here," he told Sitka. Because she'd been acting unusual, he looped her leash quickly around the edge of the bench, knotting it to keep her in place.

Then he raced toward the gazebo, passing the group of parents just as the kid's grip slipped and he slid farther, hanging only by fingertips now.

Pushing his strides as hard as he could, Tate suddenly felt like he was back in Boston, chasing a suspect down a city street. But the speed he had now, after two months of chasing Sitka around practice obstacles and trails, made his Boston days seem slow.

He reached the gazebo just as the boy lost his grip with a pained cry.

Skidding to a stop underneath him, Tate braced himself as he threw his arms out.

The boy landed awkwardly, smacking Tate in the face and sliding half out of his grasp. But Tate broke his fall and was able to set him on his feet without injury.

"Thank you, thank you, thank you," said a man who had to be the boy's father.

The boy had been fairly calm but burst into tears as his dad scooped him up.

Tate's heart rate slowed as the other parents reached them, clapping him on the back and hugging their own kids even as they admonished them not to climb the gazebo.

He smiled and accepted the accolades. He was turning back toward Sabrina and Sitka when Sabrina's shocked scream burst through the relieved voices. Sitka's panicked yelp followed.

A big green truck was rolling backward and at a slight angle down Main Street, rapidly picking up speed. It was headed right for Sitka.

His dog was straining against her leash, but he'd tethered her too well to the bench.

Tate started running again, pushing himself as hard as he could, but he was too far away. He'd never be able to get back to her in time, let alone unhook her.

Dread, guilt and anger slammed through him like a punch to the chest, then doubled as Sabrina raced in front of the truck to help his dog. He was about to lose them both. And there was nothing he could do to stop it.

Chapter Five

Panic intensified as Tate ran faster, his frantic strides still not good enough. The truck was speeding up, the incline working against him.

Sabrina dropped into an awkward squat and worked at the leash, struggling with it as Sitka whined and pulled, probably yanking the knot even tighter.

The truck hit the grass, no difference in height from the unpaved street to slow it, and Tate's whole body jerked in response, not wanting to see Sabrina get hit. Not wanting to see Sitka get hit.

Then suddenly Sabrina shifted, unhooking the leash from Sitka's collar instead.

Sitka scampered backward, away from the oncoming vehicle.

Sabrina twisted, throwing herself to the side. She landed hard on the grass as the truck zoomed past, plowing into the bench.

The metal bench crumpled under the truck's bumper, screeching enough to raise goose bumps on Tate's arms. As the bench collapsed and split, the truck kept going, then got snagged on the twisted pieces of metal. The truck made a sputtering sound, and then the engine cut out.

"You okay?" Tate panted as he slid to a stop beside Sabrina, his gaze searching for Sitka, too.

Behind him came the gasps and shouts of

worry from the group of parents and kids, but Tate ignored them as he dropped to his knees next to Sabrina.

She rolled over and pushed up on her elbows, her arms shaking. There were grass stains streaking the front of her T-shirt and dirt on her face. "Did Sitka get out of the way?"

Woof!

His dog came running around the back of the truck. She didn't stop until she'd bumped him, knocking him off his knees and onto his butt.

"I'm sorry about the leash," he told her, burying his head in her fur for a moment, relief relaxing the tightness in his chest as he saw that she hadn't been hurt.

Then he lifted his gaze to the truck, stalled and silent. When he'd seen it moving toward Sitka, it had appeared empty. As if someone had forgotten to put on their parking brake. But was it really that simple?

Dread built up again. The truck hadn't been aimed at Sabrina. But it had been close enough to her. Could her stalker have sent it down the street?

From what he knew about stalkers, it seemed unlikely. After two years of chasing her, why would he try to kill her in such an impersonal way? Usually, when stalkers got violent, they did it up close, with a gun or a knife.

Still, he swept his gaze over the area where the truck had come from. No one was there.

Pushing himself to his feet, Tate scanned the rest of the park. All he saw were the parents and kids, looking horrified.

Sitka pivoted away from him, moving to Sabrina, and gave her a sloppy kiss across the side of her face.

Sabrina laughed, petting her. "You're welcome."

Tate held out a hand for Sabrina. "Are you okay? Do you want to have a doctor look at you?"

She put her hand in his. It was a little shaky, but there was a power in her grip as she helped him pull her up.

"No doctor. I'm fine, just a little freaked out." She glanced up Main Street, where the truck had come from. "What happened? Do you think this was an accident? Or…"

Reluctantly, Tate let go of her hand as the rest of the people in the park surrounded them.

"What happened?" The dad of the kid who'd fallen from the gazebo put a hand on Sabrina's shoulder, looking worried as he clutched the boy with his other hand.

A woman bouncing a crying baby leaned closer to Sabrina, too. "Are you okay?"

"Look at the bench!" someone else exclaimed. "Who would be so careless?"

The cacophony of voices faded into the background as Tate stepped closer to the vehicle and peered through the window. The truck was set right between Reverse and Park, the key fob in the center console. A freak accident? He'd seen it before with these old trucks, where the owner thought it was in Park, but it was actually partway to Reverse. When he glanced up Main Street, he saw no one. No panicked owner racing for the park, horrified and ashamed. But maybe they'd walked away and the truck hadn't rolled backward immediately?

Still, he couldn't take any chances, especially not when Sabrina had been nearby, when they knew her stalker was here. He stepped farther away from the crowd and pulled out his radio. Speaking quietly, he said, "A truck just plowed into a bench in the park. No one was inside the vehicle, but Sabrina Jones almost got hit." Stepping behind the truck, he read off the license-plate number, dreading the potential news that it was a rental, maybe something that would come back to a fake name.

There was surprise in Officer Nate Dreymond's voice as he replied a minute later. "That vehicle belongs to Talise Poitra."

The seventy-year-old owner of the grocery store. She'd been injured pretty severely in the bombing, even been briefly in a coma. Maybe she wasn't back to a hundred percent yet.

Tate relaxed slightly as he glanced at Sabrina,

who was hunched inward as she nodded and assured the townspeople that she wasn't hurt. Beside her, Sitka's tail was wagging as everyone took turns petting her.

"I'll walk over to the store and talk to her," Nate said. "I'll radio you once I have an update."

"Thanks." Tucking the radio back into his duty belt, Tate slipped through the crowd up to Sabrina and Sitka. "Why don't you come with me to the station, where you can clean up, and we'll take a statement?"

She nodded, looking grateful for the excuse to move away from the crowd.

"What happened?" Maria Peterson asked, clutching her three-year-old daughter tightly. A few months ago, when the park had been bombed, her husband had been injured.

"Probably just an accident," Tate said. "But we're going to investigate and make sure. Did anyone notice someone by the truck before it started moving?"

The group shook their heads and shrugged, glancing at each other, but Tate wasn't surprised. They'd all been too focused on the kid on the gazebo roof.

If this *hadn't been* an accident, someone had waited for the perfect moment.

Tate led Sabrina back toward the police station. His gaze swept the area as they walked, looking for anyone who seemed out of place, who seemed too interested in Sabrina. But besides a blonde woman facing away from him as she took pictures of the stalled truck and ruined bench, all he saw was Yura Begay.

The ex-Marine called out, "Everyone all right?"

"Yeah. Just a runaway truck," Tate replied.

"You think that's all it was?" Sabrina asked.

When he glanced at her, she was biting down on her lip, her brows furrowed. Guilt was all over her face as she ran her hand down Sitka's back.

"I hope so. But no matter what, this isn't your fault. I'm the one who tied Sitka to the bench."

"Hey, Tate?" Nate's voice crackled over the radio. "I've got an update."

"Go," Tate replied, glancing at Sabrina.

"Talise said she had her keys in her purse and that she'd put the parking brake on. She parked up past the park because she wanted the exercise. Said she's still trying to get back up to speed after the bombing."

"Is she sure about the keys?" Tate asked. "Because there was a key fob in the truck."

"I asked her to check. When she went to grab her purse from behind the counter to show me, it was open and her fob was missing. She thinks someone grabbed it sometime in the past hour."

Tate felt his jaw tensing as Sabrina went pale. But was Talise right about someone taking her keys? Or had she just forgotten them in her truck? "She have any idea who?"

"No. There are no cameras in her store. She says she was in the back for a while, dealing with inventory. Normally, she brings her purse with her back there, but this time she forgot. She said the bell over the door rang a few times, but she figured people would call out if they needed her to ring them up. No one did, and it was empty when she came back up front. She said it could have been anyone. But obviously if she's right, this person knew which vehicle belonged to Talise."

"Thanks," Tate said.

"It was my stalker." Sabrina's voice was barely above a whisper. "He was trying to kill Sitka."

HER STALKER HADN'T been trying to kill her. Not this time.

No, Sabrina felt it in her gut. If he wanted to kill her, he'd do it up close, and she'd know exactly who he was before she died. He hadn't been after her today.

It was worse than that. He'd been trying to kill Sitka. Maybe because he'd seen Sitka trying to track him from her house. Or maybe because she'd been walking with Tate, because the stalker had seen her invite Tate into her home yesterday.

She hadn't even kissed Tate. She hadn't gone on a real date with him. But somehow, her stalker had known she wanted to.

He was punishing her for it by sending a message:

I'm watching. I can get to you—or someone you care about—anytime I want. Just like Dylan.

Shivering as she yanked the curtains closed on her back windows, shutting out the view of the sun sinking below the trees, Sabrina tried to stay calm. It had been hours since one of the officers had driven her home, then done a walk-through of her house before leaving.

Police still weren't sure if the truck backing up had been a targeted attack or just a freak accident. Still, they'd promised to investigate under the assumption that her stalker could have been involved. They might have been uncertain, but she wasn't. Her stalker was here, he'd made contact, and now he was back to threatening anyone who dared to enter her life.

She hadn't heard any updates. Despite the short amount of time she'd known Tate, she knew if they'd found anything, he would have told her.

She should have run the moment she'd spotted the new note on her doorstep. It didn't matter that her stalker kept finding her. She'd let herself become too invested in her life here, too invested in the life she *could* have. And she'd let herself forget how high the stakes were.

Sabrina glanced around the little cabin. It was barely eight hundred square feet, but it was cozy and the rent shockingly cheap.

Here, for the first time since she'd left New York City and her growing career in fashion design, she was doing something she loved again. No more waitressing jobs in dingy diners. No more constantly scanning the customers, searching for a face that was vaguely familiar, that might belong to a man who wouldn't leave her alone. No more endless tension between her shoulder blades, always on high alert for harassment or an attack from someone who knew she didn't want to attract attention, who knew she probably wouldn't risk going to the police.

In Desparre, she'd dared to start designing jewelry. It was what she'd always wanted to do, but back in the city, general accessories, like belts, scarves and sunglasses, were as close as she'd come. Here, she'd used an e-commerce site, made up a name with no connection to her and given it a shot. The first sale had been thrilling. As it continued to grow, she'd started to believe this could be her future.

Would she be able to do it somewhere else so easily? With Alaska's history of gold rushes, big and small, getting the raw materials had been easier than she'd expected. The cabin's tiny second bedroom had been perfect to set up a small workspace. And the view out her back windows was endlessly inspiring.

The sharp set of raps on her door made Sabrina jump. Her hand darted immediately to the alert button around her neck, but she didn't press it. Would her stalker really knock?

He'd knocked at Dylan's house.

Or at least that's what police assumed, that Dylan had opened the door to his killer, because there'd been no sign of forced entry.

The thought refused to go away as she moved slowly toward the door, heart thumping way too fast. But Dylan hadn't had any reason to suspect the person at his door was a threat. She'd mentioned the stalker, but she hadn't gone into details. She hadn't told him to be careful. Even knowing there'd been no reason for her to think he'd be in danger, the same guilt rushed forward, stinging her eyes with old tears.

Blinking them clear, she glanced around for a weapon. Making a quick detour into the kitchen, she grabbed the cast-iron pan the owner had left behind. She hefted it to shoulder height as she approached the door. It was solid and thick, tough to open even when it wasn't locked tight with a dead bolt, and especially now when her hands still shook.

Leaning in, she peered through the peephole.

It was a woman. A blonde with perfectly smoothed hair and a lot of makeup by Desparre standards, but not far from what Sabrina was used to in New York City at a club or at the design studio.

Sabrina had no idea who she was, but she lowered the pan as she leaned back. It seemed unlikely that her stalker was a woman, and equally unlikely he'd be able to convince one to help him. As the heavy pan came down, it banged the door, and she cringed.

"Hello?" the woman called when Sabrina didn't open the door.

She frowned, wondering what the woman wanted. Not that it really mattered. She wasn't about to open up for anyone right now.

When another minute went by and Sabrina continued to ignore the raps at the door, the woman called out, "My name is Ariel Clemson. I'm a reporter for the *Desparre Daily*."

There was a long pause, as if she thought that would be enticement enough, then she added, "I saw what happened at the park earlier, and I'm hoping to do a story about it." Another pause, then a hint of frustration underneath her hopeful pitch. "You know, *Local Woman Bravely Rescues Police K-9*?"

Sabrina's heart gave a small kick of anxiety. The idea of any exposure, even in the small-town newspaper, was a bad idea. There was no telling how it might get shared or who might ultimately see it. Yes, her stalker had found her, but her family hadn't. With her stalker nearby, she didn't want them to have any idea where she was.

"If you change your mind, give me a call," Ariel said through the door, and then a business card slid underneath.

Sabrina stayed quiet, still pretending not to be

home, even though the reporter clearly knew she was, until the car backed out of her driveway.

Then she turned back into the cabin that had started to feel like a real home. She took one last look at the closed shades obscuring the view she loved, and headed into her bedroom to start packing.

Chapter Six

Was there anywhere on earth that her stalker couldn't track her?

Sabrina had been so careful when she'd come here, leaving her last hideout in Washington in the middle of the night when there'd been almost no one on the roads. She'd kept a close eye on her rearview mirror for hours, not stopping until she was well into Canada. There was no way he'd been behind her. Was there?

If he hadn't physically followed her, how had he found her here? She'd stopped all contact with friends and family, not even daring to send them letters from the road in case he was watching their mailboxes, waiting to intercept them. She'd stopped shopping at any of the places she used to love, even online. She'd quit her favorite exercise program that let her join in virtual sessions. She'd stopped working in fashion design, only recently making the jump to jewelry—still design, but a different field. She'd stopped using her social-media accounts entirely.

When the PI had first suggested she leave town, when she'd detailed the extent of the changes she wanted Sabrina to make to her life, giving up hobbies and activities that could be a way to locate her, it had all sounded excessive. It had all seemed unnecessary. Now she wondered if she'd missed something, some small piece of her former life that had given her stalker a way to locate her.

She had no idea what it was. But if he'd found her all the way in no-stoplights-in-downtown, snow-you-in-until-spring Desparre, was there anywhere she'd be safe?

Hefting a bag full of her jewelry supplies, Sabrina peered through the peephole at her truck, ready in the drive. Last night, after she'd made the decision to leave, she'd packed everything and then stared, frustrated and tense, out into the darkness. She'd been afraid to go outside. Afraid her stalker was waiting in the woods, ready to ambush her.

This was worse than any of the other tiny towns she'd stopped in over the past two years. All the other times she'd run, she'd done it because she'd gotten jumpy, started seeing every shadow as a possible threat. But she'd never received a note until Desparre.

She'd gotten too comfortable here. She'd actually started to believe she could have some semblance of a life.

Now she was back to where she'd been two years ago. Scared and alone.

It didn't matter. All that mattered was her life, and the lives of the people she cared about. It was what the PI had drilled into her when she'd told Sabrina all the things she'd have to give up if she wanted to stay safe. Back then, even knowing how real the threat was, she'd burst into tears more than once in the days leading up to her planned disappearance, hoping the police would pull out a miracle and catch him.

After all this time, she thought she'd become more hardened. But at least now that she'd made the decision to leave, she knew she could do it.

She could go back to jumping from one town to the next, one state to the next. She could go back to the tedious waitressing jobs, the sleazy hotels. She could go back to being totally alone.

Pushing an image of Tate from her mind, Sabrina willed away the fear and the frustration as she yanked open the door and scanned the area. Then she hurried to her truck, pepper spray clutched in her free hand. She dropped the bag inside, scanned the woods and hurried back to the cabin.

She hadn't run with so many belongings since she'd first slipped out of New York, in the middle of the night. Back then, she'd done it with the help of the investigator, who'd made sure she wasn't followed.

In the time since then, she'd purged more and more of the things she'd once thought she couldn't live without. Small pieces of her past that had started to feel like too much baggage or that she could get a little money for in a pawnshop.

Was it even worth bringing her jewelry supplies? Probably not, since she doubted she'd be able to continue finding the things she needed to keep up her small online business. But maybe she could sell the last of it along the way. The past few years had shown her how expensive it could get to stay invisible.

Any reputable place wanted multiple forms of ID and a credit check to rent to you. Sabrina had a fake ID and the PI had made a fake credit history to go with it. But the woman had warned her that it was always safer not to rely on it. If someone dug deep enough, they'd figure out it wasn't real. Then she'd be in legal trouble herself.

Using her real ID or her real name meant someone could run a real credit check on her. She had no idea what resources her stalker had, but if he'd managed to get a hold of her social security number, he could track her from a simple credit check. She wasn't willing to take that risk, either.

So, she'd stuck to cheap motels that didn't care who she was. She'd stuck to sleazy employers who were happy to pay her cash under the table as long as they could pay her below minimum wage.

Only in Desparre had she dared to rent. She'd stopped in the grocery store downtown, and Talise had immediately noticed a scared, exhausted outsider and tried to help. She'd introduced her to the only other person buying groceries at 8 p.m., an elderly man who was going to stay with his daughter in southern Alaska, probably indefinitely. He wasn't ready to give up his cabin, but he was willing to rent it cheaply. If she was willing to pay for each new month several weeks in advance, he wasn't interested in anything more than her word.

She'd felt guilty for taking him up on it, even knowing she'd never leave him in the lurch. Now she wrote his name on an envelope and stuffed enough for next month's rent in it, hoping he wasn't relying on the income. Eventually, Tate would figure out she'd gone, and word would get to Talise, who'd pass it on to the owner.

Lifting onto her shoulder her second and final bag, one filled with her clothes and a framed picture of her mom and brother, Sabrina glanced around the cabin one last time. Then she set the emergency button the police had given her on the table in the front hall. There was a lot she'd miss about Desparre, but she couldn't stay.

It was one thing to risk her own life to put an end to her running, to regain an existence beyond simple survival. She wouldn't risk Tate's.

She liked him, probably too much for the short time she'd known him. Yes, he was an armed police officer, but her stalker had already proven how dangerous he could be. No one had seen him slipping into Talise's truck on the street, shifting it partway to Reverse and then disappearing into the woods. What if, next time, he stood in those woods and used the gun he'd taken into Dylan's home? What if he aimed it at Tate and the officer never saw the threat coming?

She refused to be responsible for anyone else's death.

It was time to go.

TATE JERKED UPRIGHT in bed, slick with sweat, his heart pounding as though he was still trapped in his nightmare.

It had plagued him all night, waking him on and off and making him sleep later than usual. As he'd thrashed around in bed, he'd kept Sitka up, too. Periodically, she'd stood up in her dog bed in the corner and whined.

He'd reassure her, try to shake off the memories, then feel himself being sucked right back into the same nightmare of that fateful morning run five and a half years ago. He'd been jogging, pushing his body hard as his mind went over and over the payoff he'd witnessed, as he stressed over the upcoming arrests. Or at least those he'd assumed would be arrested. Not just a crime lord, but also three fellow cops. Officers he'd respected, officers he'd worked with, officers who'd once come to his aid.

Then the past and present had blended. In his dream, Sabrina had jogged up next to him, distracted him with her shy smile and the far-off look in her eyes. When the gunfire had started, he'd raced off the path and into the woods, trying to make himself a difficult target, just as he'd done back then. Knowing he was probably going to die, the same certainty he'd felt back in Boston. But in his nightmare, he'd been pulling a confused and terrified Sabrina with him, and instead of a group of cops trying to corner them, her stalker had stepped out of the woods in front of them.

He'd been huge, just a dark shadow among the trees, except for a wide, evil smile. Tate had lunged for Sabrina, trying to flatten her to the ground, but before he could reach her, he'd woken.

Over and over throughout the night, the same nightmare had plagued him.

Was it a premonition? The subconscious knowledge that he couldn't fully protect her?

Stalkers and abusers were some of the hardest threats to eliminate. The law got murky, precedent not always favoring the victims, and that personality type—a man so obsessed with controlling a woman that he couldn't let go—was often willing to give up his whole life just to hurt her.

The chance that it was just driver error that had sent the vehicle racing down the street yesterday was strong. There'd been no prints besides Talise's in the car, no cameras on the street to confirm if someone else had gotten inside. So even if Tate could figure out who the stalker was, even if he *had* been responsible, Tate couldn't prove the guy had done anything with the truck.

Whether or not he'd set the vehicle in motion, Sabrina's stalker was here. He was watching her. Was Tate risking Sabrina's life even more by convincing her to stay?

The worry gnawed at him as he kicked off his covers, then stepped out of his shorts and into the shower. The heat and steam relaxed him in a way that nothing else except a good hard run could do. Five minutes later, dressed in civilian clothes since it was his day off, Tate opened the back door for Sitka.

His small house was located on the outskirts of downtown. He'd dared to buy the home, to set down roots here, because the family friend who'd created his fake name and backstory worked for Witness Protection. He hadn't created Tate's pseudonym officially. But if anyone knew how to do it right, it was a man who'd spent two decades doing it professionally.

In the years since Tate had returned to Alaska, he'd struggled with bouts of frustration and depression, especially from not being able to see his family. He could only contact them periodically, through a complicated system that would protect his safety and theirs. He'd left behind all the friends he'd made in Boston, with no notice to anyone that he was leaving. And he'd had to start over in the Desparre PD, going through the police academy a second time, pretending to be a true rookie.

But he'd taken for granted that he was safe here in Desparre.

Sure, he'd become even more cautious, but he'd been a police officer for two years in Boston, patrolling the streets during the late-night shift. Boston's crime rate was a lot higher than Desparre's. So being safety-conscious was already a way of life. His ability to be attuned to danger was probably what had saved his life five years ago.

He'd had his moments of paranoia and fear since then, but nothing like the constant terror chasing Sabrina. She was convinced yesterday's attack had been meant for Sitka, a warning that her stalker could get to her anytime, that she shouldn't let anyone close to her.

Tate's hands fisted at how well her stalker had succeeded. He'd forced Sabrina to leave everyone she loved behind, to stay all alone for two long years. From the way she'd reacted when people had tried to talk to her in the park, he could see that she hadn't let anyone truly get close to her since leaving.

It was a common tactic of scum like domestic abusers, so why not stalkers, too? Make the target of their obsession feel vulnerable and completely alone. Make them feel that if they dared to try and get help, things would only get worse. And not just for the target but for anyone she reached out to for help or companionship.

Sabrina was going to run again.

It hit him with a certainty that stole the breath from his lungs. "Sitka," he wheezed.

His dog came running across the yard, nudging him with her nose like she knew something was wrong.

"Come on," he said, hurrying back through the house and out the front door to his truck.

She raced beside him, her head pivoted slightly toward him like she was worried. She knew this wasn't a typical work mission.

"We need to stop Sabrina from running," he told her as he opened the door for her and she hopped into the truck, then leaped over to the passenger side.

His heart thundered as he silently berated himself for not recognizing what his subconscious had been trying to tell him all night. Was he already too late?

He took the roads fast, jaw clenched and his breathing too rapid, like he was headed to a distress call knowing before he arrived that all he'd be able to do was clean up the mess. If she'd already left, he had no idea how to even begin to search for her.

Based on what she'd told him about leaving New York, she'd done everything right. How the hell was her stalker still tracking her?

After what had almost happened to Sitka, she was unlikely to reach out to police again for help. She'd just keep hoping to outrun her stalker, to simply survive. But if he could track her here, how would she ever lose him? Eventually, a stalker this obsessed wouldn't be content with simply watching and leaving notes. Eventually, he'd try to make her his own. And when that inevitably failed, he'd kill her.

A sharp pain sliced through Tate's chest, and he hit the gas harder, making Sitka give a sharp bark as she hunkered low on the seat.

"Sorry, Sitka." She was used to fast driving in the police SUV, but that was better designed for her than the front seat of his truck.

He raced up the dirt road leading to Sabrina's house, and then his heart gave a little kick when he spotted taillights in her drive. Sabrina? Or someone else?

He didn't slow until he'd swung into the driveway, effectively blocking whoever was in that vehicle from escaping. Then, he hit the brakes hard, apologizing to Sitka as she yelped and righted herself again.

The brake lights on the old truck in the drive flashed and then stayed lit for a long moment, until the car turned off and Sabrina stepped out.

She crossed her arms over her chest, glancing repeatedly at the woods as she approached.

When he rolled down the window, she demanded, "What are you doing?"

"What are *you* doing?" he shot back. "We agreed that the Desparre PD would help you, Sabrina. No more running. So why are you sneaking away without even a goodbye?"

As the angry words burst from his mouth, he realized how much the idea hurt. They barely knew each other, but he'd felt an instant connection. He admired her strength and determination, the way she was willing to make sacrifices to keep the people she loved safe. He liked the way her eyes lit up when she gave him a real smile, the silly jokes she made about Sitka patrolling. He liked *her* and the idea of her not being in Desparre just felt wrong.

She frowned back at him, then her gaze darted briefly to Sitka, before returning to his. "It's one thing for me to make a stand and try to put an end to what's happening to me. I've lived with this threat for a long time, and I'm willing to take that risk to get my life back. And believe me, I want the help. But this is my fight. And now it seems like he's targeted Sitka. I'm not going to let anyone else get hurt because of me."

"We're trained for this," he insisted, trying to push his personal feelings to the background. "This threat is never going to just go away. We have to stop it."

She seemed to pale at his words, but her jaw clamped down, and she shook her head again.

Turning off his engine, he stepped out beside her. Before he could shut the door, Sitka was out, too, sitting next to Sabrina and looking up at her as if to say *I'm off duty. Pet me, please.*

A ghost of a smile flitted across Sabrina's face as she complied.

"Sabrina."

When she met his gaze again, fear and determination there, he said, "You don't want to spend your life running from this threat. I'm not going to let you do that. We're going to eliminate it."

He tried to infuse his words with certainty. It was his duty to protect her, to help her feel safe again, so she could finally regain her life fully, something he'd probably never have himself.

He couldn't stop himself from reaching out and taking her hand in his, couldn't help himself from wanting to step a little closer, to wrap his arms around her.

Duty was only part of it, he realized. He was falling for Sabrina Jones…if that was even her real name. He didn't want to lose her.

She stared up at him, warring emotions on her face, until finally she nodded. "Okay, I'll stay. Just promise me that you're all going to be careful. If this guy turns his focus on you and Sitka and you can't find him, I want you to be honest with me. I want you to tell me, so I can make my own decision about whether to stay or go."

He nodded, not breaking eye contact. "I promise."

But he knew it wasn't a promise he could keep. This wasn't a fight he was letting her take on alone anymore.

One way or another, they were going to end this here.

Chapter Seven

"Are you sure about this?" Sabrina asked as she let him into her cabin.

In response, he picked up the emergency button she'd left on the front-hall table and slipped it over her head.

She tried not to visibly react as his hands skimmed her neck, lifting her hair out of the way so the thin chain could lie underneath. But even after he removed his hands, his touch lingered, making her neck tingle.

The scent of sandalwood—his aftershave maybe—drifted toward her, intoxicating. This close, she saw how purely deep brown his eyes were, no variation to distract from the intensity of his gaze. Her breath caught, and the tingling in her neck spread down her arms and across her back.

His gaze lingered on hers, and the desire she felt was reflected back at her, beneath a layer of anxiety and concern. The corners of his lips tipped up slightly, making her want to step forward, lean into him and see what happened.

Then Sitka stepped between them, tail wagging, and broke the spell.

Sabrina laughed, releasing some of the tension both from the situation and her proximity to Tate.

She leaned down and pet Sitka, giving her pulse a chance to calm.

Then she straightened and asked, "If you're sure this is the right move, how do we find him? And are you sure you should even be here right now?" Her gaze dropped to Sitka, then rose to Tate. "I'm pretty sure he targeted Sitka because he saw you here."

Because he thinks you could be important to me, Sabrina didn't add. *The problem is, he could be right.*

A pair of vertical grooves appeared between Tate's eyebrows, marring his perfectly smooth skin. He nodded slowly. "I still think this could have been a badly timed accident. But if it wasn't, then yeah, that makes sense. Anyone who might be an ally to you, anyone who might be a friend, he sees as a threat. Competition."

Competition. Sabrina couldn't help her indignant snort, but it quickly turned into a familiar angry frustration. She'd spent two years as the object of some man's unrequited obsession, and he thought it was his right to destroy everything in her life so he could have her for himself.

"I know," Tate said softly, as if he could read her mind. "It's unfair."

Unfair was too simple a word for this. It was more than just unfair that she'd been forced to give up seeing her family and friends again, possibly for the rest of her life. That she had to take low-key jobs so she could stay below the radar. That she never felt truly safe, all because some man she might never have even spoken to thought his right to want her was greater than her right to live the life she wanted.

"Tell me," Tate said softly, compassion in his eyes. "Tell me what you're thinking."

"I just..." She sighed, looked away. She'd grown up with a strong single mom who'd worked hard to raise her and her younger brother. A mom who'd never sugarcoated the dangers women faced in the world or the inequities. Still, she'd always felt loved, supported, protected, *safe*.

Until her stalker had shown up. He was someone she might have smiled at once politely. Someone she might have had a brief conversation with at a kiosk or never spoken to at all. Someone who lived in the shadows because he was too much of a coward to tell her who he really was.

She didn't realize she'd clenched her hands into tight fists until Tate's hands were over hers, loosening them. Shifting her gaze back to him, she pulled her hands free and missed the contact immediately. "Police in New York said my stalker probably wasn't anyone identifiable in my life. They think he was somewhere on the outskirts, that I might not even recognize him at all when— if—they finally figured out who it was. But *he* has some kind of fantasy where he's essential in my life, and *I* have to live with that."

Breathing through the tears that wanted to rush forward, Sabrina said bitterly, "I can't even use my real name."

"Your name isn't Sabrina?" Tate asked softly, not sounding particularly surprised.

"It is Sabrina." The way he said her name made her suddenly glad she'd only changed her last name. She'd done it because the PI thought keeping the same first name would be easier to remember and respond to. Over the years, she'd had moments where it had felt like the only thing left in her life that was still *her*. "But it's not Jones."

His eyes narrowed slightly, and she could see him debating whether to ask what her real last name was.

"Don't," she told him. "It's better if you don't know."

He continued to stare back at her, like he might argue, until Sitka stood, spun in a quick circle and barked.

Sabrina laughed, and a grin broke out on Tate's face. "You're right, Sitka," he told her. "Maybe we should go sit down."

Realizing she'd kept him standing in the entryway a long time, Sabrina felt her cheeks heat. She turned into the house, leading him toward the living room where they'd sat before. Even though she was all packed up to disappear, the house looked mostly the same.

Seeing how small an impact she'd had on the

space in the six months she'd lived here was slightly depressing, but it was less depressing than the series of dingy hotels she'd called home before this.

Glancing around as he chose the same side of the couch he'd sat on before, Tate asked, "You want me to help you bring your stuff back in?"

Shaking her head, Sabrina sank onto the other side of the couch. Her gaze was immediately drawn into the woods. But the view that had inspired so much of her creativity now made her shiver. Was her stalker outside right this moment, seeing that his attack hadn't scared away Tate and Sitka? Was he already planning a new way to permanently remove them from her life?

Anxiety bubbled up, the certainty that she'd made a mistake letting Tate block her in. "I—"

"Don't," Tate said.

Woof! Sitka contributed, either picking up on Tate's tone or stating her own agreement. She pushed her way between Tate and the coffee table and sat in the space between them, her brown eyes intent on Sabrina.

"I feel selfish staying," she admitted softly.

"That's ridiculous." He shifted on the couch, one knee up so he was facing her. "I'm a police officer. Believe me, I've faced worse threats."

He said it like he was speaking about something specific. Sabrina couldn't help the shiver that went through her, imagining him in danger. But in law enforcement, it was part of the job.

When he'd first promised to help her get free of this threat, she'd immediately seen all the possibilities open up in her life again—possibilities like asking him on a date. But she was wrung out from two years of impending danger. How would she handle being in a relationship with a man who went to work each day anticipating danger?

"Running forever isn't the worst thing," Sabrina told him. Having police show up at Dylan's family's lake house, hearing the news that he'd been shot inside his home and then getting the note a few days later? That was the worst thing.

"No," he agreed. "But that's not your fate, Sabrina. So let's talk through some things, see if we can figure out how he found you here."

She couldn't stop herself from glancing out the window again, into the vast woods. She didn't think she'd ever see them the same way again.

"You said you haven't spoken to your family in two years, so I assume you've had no contact with anyone else, either, right? Not even this PI who helped you disappear?"

She shook her head. "No. I check her website every once in a while, to see if the New York police caught my stalker. She's supposed to leave a coded message there if it happens. In the first few months, I checked it a lot. Now I look once every month or two." Was there some way to look at her site and see where people accessed it from? "You don't think he's somehow tracking me from that, do you?"

"No. What about jobs, hobbies?"

Sabrina sighed, shook her head. "The PI I hired was good. And expensive. She worked with a skip tracer to help me disappear. What it boiled down to was basically that I needed to change everything about my life to stay safe."

Something flickered in his eyes at her words, something more than sympathy.

"Back in New York, I was a fashion designer. Accessories," she added, when he looked surprised. "Here, I've been selling jewelry I make over an e-commerce site. It's the closest I've come to normal, but it's a pretty different field."

"What did you do in all the places you lived in between?"

"Waitressing. I picked cheap diners or places near highways that were open all night and catered to truckers. Places that didn't want an employment check or actual ID."

His lips tightened into an angry line. "Places where they could pay you under the table in cash, which means they didn't bother giving you a living wage."

"Yeah," she agreed. "But I could manage on the money." Anxiety twisted in her belly, remembering what had made that year and a half before Desparre so unbearable. "It was the other threats."

The anger on Tate's face shifted into a deeper fury. "From the people working at these places? Because they saw you as part of a vulnerable population, someone with no real ID who wouldn't dare go to the police about anything illegal?"

"Sometimes," she agreed, because at almost every place she'd worked, dodging someone's hands as she served food had started to feel normal. "Sometimes it was the customers, because these places weren't exactly in the safest areas. And I'd take any shift I could get, which usually meant nights."

Her mouth suddenly went dry, thinking of all those nights rushing to her crappy car after a shift, usually in a parking lot where they didn't care about safety lighting. More than once, she'd used pepper spray on a customer who'd tried to corner her, even one who'd tried to drag her into his long-haul truck.

That had been one of the scariest moments of her life, second only to the moment she'd realized Dylan's death was because of her. She'd been exhausted after a long shift and fitting the key in the twenty-year-old junker she'd been driving in Iowa when goose bumps had erupted across her neck. She'd already had her pepper spray out because she'd learned the hard way that she needed it. As she'd spun around, lifting that spray, fear had exploded. The guy was huge, well over six feet and at least twice her weight. It might not have all been muscle, but it didn't matter. She'd barely started to depress the trigger on her pepper spray before he swatted the canister away like he was swatting a fly.

She'd choked on the fumes, but he'd just coughed and slapped a hand over her mouth, as if there was anyone around to hear her scream or care if they had. His other arm had yanked her flush against him, shoving her face into his sweat-stained T-shirt. It had been hard to breathe as he'd dragged her, ignoring the fists she'd slammed into his arms and the one solid kick she'd gotten to his knee, like he barely felt them.

He'd loosened his grip slightly to open the door of his truck, and she'd wrenched herself away, simultaneously flinging a desperate punch. She'd gotten lucky as he'd twisted back toward her and her punch had landed right on his prominent Adam's apple. He'd gagged and she'd run.

She'd gotten in her car and raced out of that town, out of Iowa. She'd never had such a close call again, but it had been a tough reminder: her stalker wasn't the only threat out there.

"I've been careful," she told Tate, trying to shake off the remnants of that memory. "He shouldn't have been able to track me here. I've changed cars. I've lived in eight different states before coming to Alaska."

Frustration bubbled up, stronger than it had been in a long time, because she'd actually started to hope again. "So how the hell did he find me here?"

TATE RAN UP the hill outside Desparre's downtown at a punishing pace, let the steady rhythm of his pounding feet calm his fury.

Sabrina had almost left. If he'd been seconds later, she'd have been gone, and he wouldn't have been able to find her.

The idea hurt a lot more than it should have and Tate tried not to focus on why. Because right now, his feelings for her didn't matter. Only her safety did.

Gritting his teeth, he pushed himself harder, his chest heaving as he finally crested the hill. He was alone, having dropped Sitka off at home after they'd left Sabrina's cabin. Sitka liked to run with him, but when he was in this kind of mood, he never brought her along. There was no reason to punish her for his bad mood.

Bending over, Tate rested his palms on his knees as his heart rate slowed. Then he straightened and peered over the edge of the hill. If downtown Desparre was sleepy, the outskirts were damn near comatose. There were lots of places to get lost in nature. A boon for locals who knew the area and the safety precautions. Not so great for unprepared tourists looking for adventure. Or for a cop who'd been ambushed on a quiet trail.

These days, though, he didn't constantly scan his surroundings on his run. The impulse was still there, but he tried to resist. It was a slippery slope from appropriate caution to paranoia.

When Sabrina had shared some of her experience, he'd wanted to open up about his own. He'd wanted to tell her he knew exactly what it was like to have someone come after you. Sure, the reasons and methods were different. The outcome, too. But the terror of that moment in the park would never fully go away. The nightmare he'd had last night was rare, but the fear was always in the back of his mind.

One of the officers who'd tried to kill him was in prison. The moron had actually used his police-issued weapon to shoot Tate, so when the bullet had been dug out of Tate's arm, that had cinched Officer Jim Bellows's fate. But the other two had gotten off. Not enough evidence, the jury had ruled. Not enough evidence that they'd participated in the payoff, and not enough evidence that they'd participated in the attempt on Tate's life.

Tate had only seen Jim in the park. But Jim wasn't the only officer there, Tate was sure. Jim must have brought his two closest friends on the force, Paul Martin and Kevin Fricker. Tate had seen all three take the payoff, but financial forensics had only found a large deposit to Jim Bellows.

It was no surprise that the other two had used throwaway weapons or that they'd hidden the money better. Jim had always been a liability, constantly on the verge of an Internal Affairs investigation for one reason or another. Usually his inability to curb his drinking, since he'd shown up intoxicated at work a few times.

Kevin and Paul were smarter, more cautious. It had turned out they were just as crooked.

Still, Kevin and Paul had managed to stay on the force, at least for a time. But Tate's accusations had stained their reputations, as well as his own. The rest of the officers hadn't known who to believe, or who to trust. Eventually, Kevin and Paul had left—and so had Tate.

The court had decided Kevin and Paul hadn't been involved. The feds decided they weren't an ongoing threat. But Tate knew otherwise. The last thing Kevin had whispered as he'd walked past Tate on his final day at the police station had been "Jim was my best friend, and you destroyed his life. Watch your back. One day, we might just destroy yours."

Tate hadn't bothered to tell the FBI about the threat. The case had been closed. And a vague threat wasn't enough to reopen anything.

Instead, he'd contacted an old family friend and asked what it would take to disappear. Until that moment, he'd expected to stay in Boston. Even though the other officers hadn't gone to jail, the fact that he'd accused them would make them immediate suspects if any harm came to him. But the look in Kevin's eyes had told Tate he wasn't the only one in danger.

Now, staring down into the town he'd grown to love so much, the town that sometimes made him wonder why he'd ever left Alaska in the first place, Tate wished he'd seen it coming. Some of the signs were there, but until he'd stumbled onto the three cops taking a payoff, he never would have guessed it was happening.

Before the incident, Jim Bellows had seemed like a time bomb. Kevin and Paul had seemed more even-keeled, more professional. They were partners and had actually come to Tate's aid on a dangerous call once. Still, he'd always seen something volatile in them, something vague that made him intuitively understand why they'd befriended Jim.

One of the lieutenants used to call Paul *Napoleon* because he made up for being five foot six by lifting weights until he resembled a tank. The officer had always loved to intimidate with his size. Kevin, who looked a solid decade younger than his thirty-nine years, used the fact that he *wasn't* particularly intimidating—even at six foot four—to get close to someone. Then he'd bring the hurt.

Both tactics were fine, in the appropriate situation. But Tate preferred to stick to tactics that didn't have an undercurrent of bullying.

He hadn't destroyed their careers fully. Both had gone on to other departments in other cities. But he doubted he'd happened to catch them taking their first payoff. What he probably *had* destroyed was their illegal-income source. And that day, Tate had known they'd never forgive him for that. Or for putting Jim behind bars.

So, when his family friend had said he could do unofficially for Tate what he'd done for years for federal witnesses—only to a lesser degree, giving Tate some contact with his family—he'd jumped on it. Better to start over than to constantly live in fear. Especially if that fear was for more than just himself.

In the years since, he'd kept tabs on Kevin and Paul, expecting one day their illegal activities would catch up to them. But they were both still police officers, both still a potential threat. He'd finally accepted that this was his life now and allowed himself to embrace it.

He would probably never go home again. But he was going to make sure that wasn't Sabrina's fate.

Chapter Eight

Someone was staring at her.

Sabrina's breathing became shallow as the certainty washed over her. She glanced around the little downtown, trying to be subtle but feeling obvious as her gaze lingered on any man she didn't recognize as a longtime Desparre resident.

Maybe she just sensed the police watching her.

Tate had told her that the police wanted her to act normal, try to get out and engage with people. She was supposed to notify them whenever she went anywhere, so they could watch from a distance. They figured that's what her stalker was doing, so they would look for anyone paying her too much attention.

As she glanced around, Officer Lorenzo Riera nodded briefly at her. It evened out her breathing, made her shoulders relax from where they'd crept up her neck. If she couldn't have Tate watching over her—she knew he was off duty today—having the serious veteran officer keep watch was a close second.

Walking from where she'd parked near the grocery store toward the park felt strange today. She'd done this walk many times, but somehow, even after doing it just once with Tate and Sitka, it felt unnatural not to have them at her side.

Every step felt stiff, and the swing of her arms

that was meant to look casual seemed awkward. No matter how many times she told herself not to make it obvious she was watching for someone, she couldn't stop herself from scanning the area.

A tall man with dark hair and a terrible mustache stood up the hill, near a vehicle that was parked close to where Talise's truck had been yesterday. He met her gaze and gave her a brief nod the same way Officer Riera had done. But this man wasn't a cop.

She didn't know him. The way he immediately averted his gaze after that nod made her shoulders tense up again. Was the bad mustache a disguise? She didn't recognize him from around town, but then again, she didn't know everyone.

Her gaze went back to the officer, to see if he'd noticed, but his expression was even. He didn't even seem to be paying attention to her as he meandered across the street, stopping to chat with people along the way.

She tried to will Officer Riera to look her way as the mustached man got into a light-colored sedan, but the officer still wasn't watching. So, she picked up her pace, hoping to get a license-plate number. As the vehicle pulled onto the street quickly enough to make the tires squeal, she saw that the plate was caked over with mud.

Frustrated, she glanced back at the officer again.

This time, he looked in her general direction,

his gaze sweeping over and past her. As he continued walking, he shook his head.

Did that mean he knew the man? Was she being paranoid? Seeing every man as a threat now?

She reached for her phone to text the officer, to make sure he'd seen what she had.

"Sabrina!"

She jumped at the sound of her name, almost dropping her phone as her hand jerked automatically toward her purse, where she still kept a canister of pepper spray.

When her gaze swung toward the park, she saw Lora Perkins and Adam Lassiter waving. Lora was frowning, like she knew something was wrong, and Adam seemed like he was faking enthusiasm at seeing her.

After Talise, they were some of the people she knew best in Desparre. So, she tucked her phone away and pasted on a smile she could feel quivering as she walked toward them.

"Are you okay?" Lora asked, putting a hand on her arm when she reached them. "We heard about the truck almost hitting you yesterday."

Sabrina nodded. "Yeah. The police think it was a freak accident." It was what they'd said to tell anyone who asked about it, just in case her stalker had been responsible. They wanted him to feel like he'd gotten away with it, so he'd be more confident continuing to follow her. Talise had been asked to play along, pretend she couldn't believe she'd forgotten to engage her parking brake. Police hadn't given her specifics on why, just that they thought the ploy would help draw out the person responsible.

Lora's frown deepened, the perfectly smooth, pale skin on her forehead furrowing as if she could tell Sabrina was lying.

Lora was only a few years older than Sabrina, but from the moment they'd met, she'd mothered Sabrina. She'd even commented on it once, laughingly telling Sabrina she knew she was doing it, but that she couldn't help it. She'd grown up in the mountains of Desparre, with drug-addicted parents and three younger siblings who needed to be fed and cared for. They were all adults now, all successful and married and living far away from the town where they'd grown up. While Lora claimed she couldn't bring herself to have kids and spend the rest of her life the way she'd spent her childhood—looking after others—she couldn't seem to stop herself from doing it with everyone she met.

"Are you sure?" Adam asked.

Sabrina's gaze shifted to him. He, too, was a few years older than her. He was newer to Desparre than she was and knew even fewer people. He probably never would have spoken to her or anyone else if Lora hadn't pressured him to do it. Once you befriended Lora, it was hard to say no to her good-natured attempts to help.

He didn't seem particularly suspicious of her lie, but it was hard to tell beneath the look of despair and grief that was always on his face. His wife had died a few months earlier, and he'd left behind their home on the other side of Alaska for some peace and quiet here.

She shrugged, trying to sound flippant. "Yeah, what else would it be? It was scary, but trust me, Talise will never forget to put her parking brake on again!"

Adam nodded, his gaze drifting to the other side of the park, where a group of kids were playing. But Lora still looked suspicious.

Sabrina averted her gaze, and her attention caught on a man standing by the park gazebo. He was lowering his phone like he'd had it up to take a picture, and his gaze locked on hers, lingering for a moment before he turned and walked out of the park.

Her breath caught. Something about his build and his walk was familiar. From seeing him around town? Or from back in New York?

"Sabrina." Lora squeezed her arm. "Are you sure you're okay? You seem really spooked."

Ripping her gaze away and hoping Officer Riera was paying attention, Sabrina tried for a smile. Because it shook way too much to be believable, she admitted, "I guess yesterday scared me more than I realized. I keep thinking a car is going to come at me out of nowhere."

She tried for a laugh and was amazed when it came out self-deprecating but real. "I think I'm going to head home and relax for a while."

"That's probably a good idea," Lora said.

"Let us know if you need anything," Adam added.

The look on his face—like he'd finally lifted out of his own grief enough to see something around him was wrong—told her this wasn't working at all.

She needed to get it together. Because the best way to find her stalker was to give him a chance to watch her. And give the police a chance to spot him doing it.

The way things were going, she was more likely to alert him to the fact that police were watching. And if he knew that, would he leave? And leave her in a perpetual state of limbo?

Or would he make one last bold move and kill *her* this time?

Tate stared at the picture of Dylan Westwood on his computer screen. This was Sabrina's old boyfriend. It had to be.

Leaning back in his chair in the second bedroom he used as a home office, Tate studied the man Sabrina had been dating two years ago. He'd woken early to do some digging into Sabrina's life, but he only had another hour and a half until he needed to be at work.

The photo someone had chosen to accompany Dylan's obituary showed him grinning, amusement clear in his dark blue eyes. According to the obit, the twenty-eight-year-old marketing associate at a record label had been survived by both parents and four younger siblings.

Tate had found the obituary from cross-referencing an article about Dylan's murder from New York two years ago. He'd found *that* article by searching for information about a murder in that time frame that mentioned a stalker. Dylan had been shot in his own home and the story said police believed his girlfriend's stalker had murdered him. They were asking anyone who had information to come forward.

Sabrina Jones's real name was Sabrina Reilly.

Tate tried the name out on his lips. Something about it matched her more than Jones. But Jones was a smart choice for going on the run, since it was one of the most popular last names in the US. If she ever ran into trouble with her fake ID, it might have been easily explained away as a mix-up with some other Sabrina Jones.

Pulling up a couple of social-media sites, Tate typed in *Sabrina Reilly* and searched through the possible matches. He found her on the third site. Her account was set to private, but there were certain things he could still see, including her profile picture, which told him he'd found the right Sabrina. In the picture, her head was thrown back, and she was laughing. Her hair was shorter, still with those natural waves. Her dress was more trendy, less practical than what she wore in Alaska. But mostly, she looked the same—minus the haunted look in her eyes.

Scrolling through the posts that weren't hidden from view, including pictures she'd been tagged in—all from over two years ago—Tate searched for anything or anyone that seemed out of place. But all of the comments seemed to be from friends, and even meticulously cross-checking each of the people who'd liked her photos didn't reveal anything that stood out as odd.

So, he went deeper, checking each of the friends in those photos, until he found a few who had their profiles set to public. He dug into their older pictures, too, looking for anywhere Sabrina was not tagged or in the background, searching for anyone who commented or liked too many of them. Still nothing.

With a frustrated sigh, he kept going, finding other people with the last name Reilly, until he came across one who had to be her older brother. Conor Reilly. He was a stockbroker with a long-term girlfriend and a love of baseball. Two years ago, his posts had suddenly become public. On some of his early posts, there were multiple comments asking about his sister, all of which he'd ignored.

Tate dug into each of the people who'd asked

about her, but none seemed likely to be her stalker. They all seemed far too embedded in the Reillys' lives. And Tate agreed with the New York police: the person stalking Sabrina had to be on the outskirts of her life. If he was too close to her, she would have noticed that he paid her too much attention or that he acted extra awkward, nervous, angry or overly emotional around her.

Leaning back in his chair, Tate frowned at the screen. He felt a hint of guilt at digging into Sabrina's personal life without her permission, but if this led to a promising lead, it would be worth it. He'd learned early as a cop that people put way more of themselves online than they realized. And a lot more of it was discoverable by strangers than they probably wanted.

The missing piece he needed might still be here, somewhere, tangled in a web of loose social connections. He'd keep picking at it when he could, but for now, it confirmed what the Desparre PD had decided from the outset: the key to finding Sabrina's stalker would be tracking him here. Not trying to dig him out of her past.

Woof!

Startled, Tate glanced over and realized Sitka was standing in the doorway. "What is it, Sitka?"

She took a step forward and barked again.

Tate frowned at her, knowing she wanted his attention but not sure why. He glanced at his watch, realizing that he'd lost track of time while he'd been searching. He needed to hurry and get ready for work. Jumping to his feet, he said, "Thanks, Sitka." Then he heard the sound of a car engine starting up.

She hadn't been trying to tell him they were running late for work. She'd been alerting him that someone was here.

Hurrying down the stairs, Tate peered through his peephole out to his drive. The area around his house was partly obscured by woods, but he didn't see anyone. The car was gone. Except... He squinted at his front stoop, where something had been left.

Sabrina's stalker had obviously identified him and Sitka as allies of Sabrina. Even if he'd figured out where Tate lived, would he dare to come here?

Thinking of the description of Dylan's death from one of the articles about the unsolved murder, Tate ran upstairs, where he kept his gun locked up. Less than a minute later, he was back downstairs, phrases from the article floating through his brain.

...shot in his own home...house ransacked... only suspect is an unidentified person stalking his girlfriend.

Compared to the fingerprint-free notes the stalker left Sabrina, Dylan's murder seemed uncontrolled, full of rage.

"Sitka, move over here," Tate instructed, pointing back toward his kitchen, away from the front door.

She followed his instructions, backing quickly into the kitchen. But she was looking at him like she didn't understand. They weren't working; they were at home. Home was safe and fun.

He didn't think anyone was out there, but he didn't want to take any chances if the stalker had left some kind of explosive device or wanted to lure him closer.

Peering through the door once more, Tate tried to identify the object, but it was right up against the door, mostly out of view. Instead of opening his front door, he told Sitka, "Stay," then ran around to his attached garage at the side and slipped out that way. He didn't see anyone skulking near his house, but then, he'd heard a vehicle drive away. So most likely, the person had dropped something at the door, then run.

Locking the door leading out of his garage behind him so no one could slip inside while he was investigating, Tate did one more sweep of the area. Then, gun raised, he crept toward the front of his house. He forced his breathing to stay deep and even, the way he would on a run. Years as a police officer helped prevent his senses from dimming into a dangerous tunnel as he scanned his surroundings. Not having a partner at his side made him extra aware of every twig breaking beneath his feet, telegraphing exactly where he was and where he was going.

When he reached the front of his house, he

blew out a surprised breath. The item leaning against his front door was a newspaper. Still not putting his weapon away, he moved closer, studying it carefully as he approached. It wasn't a copy of some New York paper like he might have expected if Sabrina's stalker wanted to send him a message, but the *Desparre Daily*.

As he reached the porch, he was sure it wasn't rigged. There was just a sticky note on it that read, *Thought you'd enjoy this!* It was signed by Ariel Clemson, a local reporter he'd helped out once.

Tucking his gun into the waistband of his pajama pants, Tate picked it up and unrolled it. His heart gave a hard thump as he read the headline: *Woman Rescues Police K-9 from Runaway Truck.*

He swore as he stared at the picture underneath the headline. The photo was grainy, taken from way down the street at an awkward angle, but there was Sabrina frantically trying to free Sitka as the truck barreled toward them. And in the background there was Tate racing to help.

Dread sank from his chest, settling low in his gut. The *Desparre Daily* was a tiny local paper, with such low distribution that they were constantly in danger of folding. But they had an online presence.

Were the officers who wanted revenge on him actively searching for him the way he'd been searching for Sabrina's stalker? Would they find this photo and consequently find him?

He flashed back to the warning from his friend who handled Witness Protection relocations: "If we think someone has been exposed, we don't wait and hope. We get them out and start over somewhere else. New name, new backstory and no contact with their last life. I recommend you follow the same protocol."

The dread he felt expanded outward. After promising Sabrina that he'd help her get her life back, would he have to desert her to save his own life?

Chapter Nine

As he came back inside his house, Tate was swearing enough to make Sitka stare up at him with concern.

He dropped to his knees in front of her and rested his head on top of hers. Although he'd adopted her and covered her everyday costs, the Desparre PD had paid thousands of dollars for their K-9 training. If he had to leave, they'd probably expect to keep her.

"What am I going to do, Sitka?" he asked softly.

She whined in response, then gave him a sloppy kiss across his chin.

The idea of leaving her behind made his chest tighten painfully. But if he took her with him, would the Desparre PD search for them? Since the safest option would be to leave without any notice or explanation, they probably would. He'd be a lot easier to track with an Alaskan Malamute at his side. Plus, if he was in danger, bringing her along would put her in danger, too.

She might be better off staying here, being placed with another officer. But Tate wasn't sure if anyone else at the station would want to become a K-9 handler. Even if they did, he doubted the station could afford more training. That meant Sitka might be paired with someone who didn't know what they were doing, who inadvertently put her in danger anyway.

He swore again, the anxiety in his gut and chest expanding as his head started to throb. Maybe he'd been a fool to get so comfortable here, to make connections that he'd ultimately have to leave. Maybe Sabrina had the right idea, trying not to get close to anyone.

Squeezing his eyes shut, Tate continued resting his head on Sitka's until she let out another whine. Knowing he was worrying her, Tate lifted his head and stroked her fur until it helped relax him enough to think clearly.

Maybe his old police chief would have an idea. Although he and Keara Hernandez had rarely talked about his past, there had been comfort in knowing he *could* go to her if the burden of his past started to impact his present.

He grabbed his cell phone off the kitchen table, then cringed as he glanced at the time while he made the call. He'd have to hurry if he wanted to be on time for work. But should he even go?

When Keara answered, Tate replied, "Hi, Keara." He cringed at the anxiety in his voice.

"What's going on?"

Trust his old police chief to get right to the point. She'd always been that way, and he was happy to see that trading in her job as police chief in tiny Desparre for a detective job in Anchorage hadn't changed her.

"I think I might have been exposed." He told her about the article.

There was a slight pause, then she asked, "How clear are you in this picture? How much detail does it give about you?"

"I'm in the background. The image is a little blurry, but my face is recognizable. And I'm named in the article—by my fake name, of course. The focus is on Sabrina and how she rescued Sitka. It's a feel-good kind of story."

"Sitka? Really? That's what you named your pup?" Keara demanded to know.

"Yeah."

"Well, I was about to say that the risk was minuscule, but that just increased it a little."

"Because someone searching for the name Tate Donnoly—" his real name "—might think to search with Sitka, Alaska," Tate realized.

"Exactly," Keara affirmed.

He'd chosen the dog's name because it had felt like a way to hold on to some small piece of his past, the place where he'd spent his childhood. It had felt like an inside joke no one knew but him. Now it just seemed reckless.

"Did your old colleagues know you grew up there?"

"I didn't talk to those guys much. But it probably wouldn't be hard to figure out if they asked around."

Keara sighed. "It's still probably a low risk

level. I'm sure these guys know you disappeared. How likely would it be for you to get another job as a police officer under an assumed name? But if you want to feel totally safe..."

"I know. But I have a life here."

"I'm sorry I'm not there to help," Keara said.

Tate smiled. "I'm not. I can tell you're enjoying being a detective again. Plus, being in Anchorage must be better than a long-distance relationship." Her boyfriend, Jax, was a Victim Specialist for the FBI in Anchorage.

"Well, there's that," Keara said, and the tone of her voice told him what was coming before she announced, "We got engaged last weekend."

"Congratulations, Keara. That's great." He tried to sound enthusiastic, because he *was* happy for her. If anyone deserved it, it was his old chief, who'd come to Alaska to escape memories of her husband's murder. But he couldn't help the tinge of jealousy that came with it. Would he ever be in a place where he'd feel safe enough to let someone in his life that way?

"Look," Keara said, her voice back to serious. "It's pretty unlikely those officers would dig this article up. But there's no guarantee. If it was me, I'd be cautiously patient. But, Tate, you need to get ready to run. I can try to help you. Jax isn't an investigator, but maybe he can talk to his colleagues at the FBI, help you disappear."

"No," Tate said. Right now, he was using a

name illegally. He was acting as a police officer under a false name, too, and if it ever came out that Keara had known it, he wouldn't be the only one facing legal action. "If I need to disappear again, I'll do it alone."

There was another pause, and Tate knew that even though Keara would risk her own life to help him, she had to be relieved he wouldn't ask her to do it. "Keep me informed, if you can."

"I will."

"And, Tate? Watch your back, okay?"

"Yeah," he agreed, saying goodbye. He hoped it wasn't the last time he'd talk to her.

He hoped this newspaper article wasn't the beginning of the end of his time as Tate Emory.

SABRINA STARED AT the headline of the *Desparre Daily* that Adam Lassiter handed her when she ran into him later that afternoon at the grocery store, dread clenching her chest.

"You're a hero," Adam said, looking surprised that she wasn't excited. "You rescued a K-9."

She offered a wan smile, then glanced at the article. It was written by Ariel Clemson, the woman who'd shown up on her doorstep the other day. Apparently, she'd decided she didn't need Sabrina's input to tell the story.

As she stared at the slightly blurry photo, she remembered a woman standing off in the distance that day, snapping pictures after Sabrina had jumped out of the way of the truck. At the time, she'd thought the woman had simply been a gawker. She'd turned her head, hoping the images wouldn't be plastered on social media.

Looking at Adam, she asked, "How many people get this paper?"

He shrugged, reminding her that he hadn't lived here all that long. "I have no idea. I doubt very many. I mean, I came to Desparre because I figured I was more likely to run into a moose than another person most days." He flushed, then added, "Not that I mind talking to you. I just—"

"I understand," Sabrina said softly. She hadn't shared with anyone that she'd come here after losing a boyfriend to violence, but she'd been tempted to share a sanitized version with Adam because he was clearly so lost since his wife's death a few months earlier.

"Yeah." Adam looked away, probably thinking she was just trying to be supportive. "Well, anyway, I thought you might want the paper. I already bought it." He hefted his bags of groceries, then nodded goodbye.

After he was gone, Sabrina read the article more closely. It was heavy on drama, a firsthand report of watching the vehicle slide out of control. It detailed Sabrina's "heroic" determination to free the town's new police K-9, a dog Ariel described as "a town treasure."

Sabrina's amusement faded as she got to the

section that described the incident as "suspicious," saying police were investigating the possibility that it had been targeted. Ariel hadn't mentioned *who* police thought the attack had targeted, however.

"Sabrina!"

Her head jerked up at the sound of her name, and she tried to smile as Lora hurried toward her.

"I see you read the paper!"

"Yeah." Sabrina folded it into her purse to look at more closely later. "How many people see this paper?"

Lora laughed, a rich, hearty sound that sounded like it belonged to a much bigger woman than the barely five-foot-tall Lora. "I never took you for a fame hound! Sorry to say, not very many. I think our population is *maybe* five hundred. And that's including all the recluses up the mountain who avoid everyone and I doubt are keeping up with local news. But it is online."

Online. Of course it was. Sabrina gritted her teeth to keep from swearing.

"What's wrong? You don't like the fame?" Realization washed over Lora's face, and she lowered her voice. "You're running from something, aren't you, honey? I should have realized. So many of the people in this town are."

She put a hand on Sabrina's upper arm and squeezed lightly. "Don't worry. The *Desparre Daily* website is poorly run. It goes down at least once a month, and you'd really have to search hard to find it. Besides, I'm guessing *Sabrina Jones* isn't your real name?"

Sabrina shrugged, not wanting to lie to one of the few people she'd dared to call a friend since going on the run. But she wasn't about to tell her the truth, either.

Lora squeezed her arm again. "This is a pretty remote spot. Someone would have to be *really* determined to track you down here."

Sabrina mustered up another smile, and this one must have been more convincing, because Lora smiled.

Patting her arm once more, she said, "Try not to worry. No one's going to use that tiny little article to track you down."

Sabrina hoped it was true. Because her stalker might have already found her, but he wasn't the only one she wanted to stay hidden from.

Her family loved her. They hadn't wanted her to go. She'd bet a lot of money that both Conor and her mom searched for her still. And she didn't want them to find her, didn't want them to be in any danger like Dylan. If they did, it would defeat most of the purpose of her leaving.

Glancing up as a young officer whose name she couldn't remember entered the grocery store and gave her a subtle nod, Sabrina hoped the Desparre PD found her stalker soon. Because no matter how small the risk of exposure was with this article, she wasn't willing to take chances with her family's safety.

It was definitely time to figure out a contingency plan.

Chapter Ten

A day after her picture had shown up in the paper, people were still yelling out, "Great job!" and "Thanks for saving our K-9!" when she walked around. But the newspaper's online site had been down most of the day, and she hoped it would stay that way. Hoped the only people who'd ever hear about her supposed heroics were Desparre locals.

She'd acted on instinct that day in the park, and she'd do it again. But she could do without the attention.

Stepping out of her old truck, she couldn't help but glance around for the man who'd put her in the paper. Whoever he was, he wasn't obviously staring. Hopefully today they'd identify him.

She walked into the police station and Officer Nate Dreymond rose from the front desk and opened the door to let her into the area marked *Police Only.*

"Good luck," he told her.

"Thanks," she said as she walked through and immediately spotted Tate and Sitka.

Tate smiled at her, a soft smile that somehow managed to be perfectly professional but still completely directed at her.

It made her pulse pick up, and her feet followed suit. When she reached his side across the open-concept space a minute later, he asked, "What's

it like being a local hero?" But something in his
eyes told her the newspaper article bothered him
as much as it did her.

"You saw that?"

Woof! Sitka contributed.

The dog's tail thumped the floor when Sabrina
looked at her, and Sabrina grinned and pet her.

"The reporter left a copy on my doorstep. I forgot that she lived near me. I helped her when she
thought someone was sneaking around her house
last year and mentioned that I lived close in case
she was in trouble. Apparently, she remembered."

Sabrina felt a brief, ridiculous spurt of jealousy
that she pushed aside. "So you think we can find
this guy today?" She heard the hopeful note in
her voice and realized that it felt different than it
had in a long time.

The fact that the stalker hadn't left her a note
or tried anything else since he'd sent that truck
speeding toward them three days ago made her
wonder if he'd noticed that police were always
around and he'd fled. For once, she prayed he
hadn't, prayed he'd stick around long enough to
get caught.

"I'm ready to look at those pictures."

Tate had called her that morning, letting her
know the officers who'd been watching over her
the past couple of days while she walked around
town had managed to get pictures of men who
might be paying too much attention. She'd been

shocked; she hadn't noticed any of the officers taking pictures. But then she'd felt a surge of hope. Maybe she'd recognize someone. Maybe this two-year-long nightmare would actually have an end.

"Let's do it, then," Tate said, leading her into a conference room with a long table where the chief of police was waiting.

Sitka followed, too, pushing past her to stand next to Tate at the far end of the table.

The police chief stood. "How are you feeling, Sabrina?"

She gave a smile. "Hopeful."

Chief Griffith smiled back at her. "Me, too. My officers got a lot of pictures." At the look she must have given him, he laughed and said, "Don't worry. We didn't notice tons of people watching you. But someone skilled who has practice stalking gets good at blending in, at appearing like he's *not* watching you. We took pictures of anyone around you."

"Oh." She heard the surprise in her voice. Police in New York had tried hard to locate and catch her stalker. She knew they had. But this was a whole different level.

The same hope sparked again, a little stronger this time, as she took a seat where the chief indicated. On the table in front of her was a folder.

"Take a look at the pictures in there," Chief Griffith said. "We printed them out and blew them up to make it easier. Take as much time as you want. You don't need to be certain. If you think you recognize anyone from New York or if you've seen anyone in places you wouldn't expect—near your house or around you more than once—let us know. It might just be that we're a small town, but we'd rather check it out. Even if you're just getting a weird vibe from someone, point him out. Okay?"

She nodded, opening the folder as Tate sat next to her and Sitka pushed her way between the chairs to sit beside her, too.

Sabrina smiled at her and paused to pet the sweet dog. "Thanks, Sitka," she whispered. It might have been her imagination, but it felt like the dog knew she was nervous and was trying to support her.

Then she started flipping through the photos. She stopped periodically to study some more closely, but she didn't remember any of the people in them hanging around her in Desparre. And she definitely didn't remember any of them from New York.

She paused on an image from two days ago, when she'd been heading toward the park. One of the photos had captured the man she'd seen standing beside a car parked right near where Talise's had been before it came racing toward Sitka. Even in the photo, the way he was looking toward her made her shiver. Just like it had when she'd first seen it, his mustache seemed out of place on his face, as if it was some kind of disguise. She pointed at him and looked over at Tate, then Chief Griffith.

Tate shook his head. "That's Shawn. I don't remember his last name, but he lives one town over, in Luna, and has for at least four years. He comes into Desparre pretty regularly. He's kind of antisocial, but there's no way he was stalking you in New York two years ago."

Her shoulders dropped. Was this all for nothing?

She flipped to the next photo, and her anxiety sparked again as she looked past herself, Lora and Adam talking, to a guy in the background watching them from near the gazebo. "What about this guy? I thought he might have taken a picture of me that day."

Tate frowned at the photo, leaning closer and giving her a whiff of the same sandalwood scent she'd noticed the day he'd come to her house to stop her from leaving Desparre. It was a scent she'd started to associate entirely with him, a scent that made her want to breathe more deeply.

"I don't know this guy." He looked behind him. "Chief?"

Sabrina passed the picture over and then watched as the police chief studied it carefully and finally shook his head. "No. And it does look like he might be trying to hide. I'll check with the other officers and see if anyone else recognizes him."

Was this him? Hope started to build again, with whiplash intensity, and Sabrina met Tate's gaze, knowing that hope was reflected in her eyes.

As he gazed back at her, the rest of the room, the chief, the pictures all seemed to fade into the background. All she could focus on was Tate, on the sharp angles of his face and the fullness of his lips. On the way his dark hair swept over his forehead and the hypnotizing deep brown of his eyes. Her breathing went shallow as a familiar spark ignited inside her, one she'd been feeling more and more often when she was around him. The way his gaze seemed to intensify on her said he felt it, too.

But if the man in the picture *was* her stalker and they could finally end this threat, she'd be leaving. Trying to begin a long-distance relationship all the way from New York while she was trying to reintegrate into her old life wasn't practical, even if Tate was interested. If they finally found her stalker, she'd never get the chance to see if her growing interest in Tate could have become something.

"DOES ANYONE RECOGNIZE this man?" Tate asked, holding up the photo Sabrina had identified earlier. She'd gone home, and Tate had felt a sudden pull to go with her, to stay beside her, but he had hours of work left today.

The few other officers inside the police station stopped their work and came to look.

Veteran officer Charlie Quinn, a gruff guy who looked a lot older than his forty-two years, squinted at it for a long moment, then finally shook his head. "He looks vaguely familiar, but I don't know him. If he's a local, he must not come around town much."

It was a problem they'd run into before in investigations. Desparre was a small town in terms of population, but large when it came to acreage. So, while locals tended to recognize each other, if someone wanted to hide, they definitely could. In fact, one of Tate's earliest cases on the Desparre PD had involved a couple of kidnappers who'd hidden out in the mountains for years without anyone realizing.

Charlie's partner, Max Becker, pushed his way through. "Let me see."

Max was a few years older than Tate and had been on the force a few years longer. He was brash and seemed to think there was no space in a professional setting for friendships, but he got the job done.

He stared at the picture for less time than Charlie had, then shook his head, too. "Nah, I don't know him."

"Nate?" Tate called into the front of the station.

The youngest officer on the force, who'd recently turned twenty, hurried into the bullpen.

"You recognize this guy?" Tate asked hopefully. Nate might have been relatively new to the force, but he'd lived in Desparre all his life.

Nate's lips pursed as he leaned close to the photo, making Max snicker. "Try not to go cross-eyed."

Ignoring him, Nate hedged. "Maybe. He does look a little familiar, but I don't think he's local." Straightening, he asked, "You think this is Sabrina's stalker?"

"Maybe. Any idea when you might have first seen him?"

Nate frowned, creating lines across his pale, freckled forehead. "Not that long ago, actually. Maybe a month or two?"

"You ready to go?" Lorenzo Riera called to Nate as he came into the bullpen.

"Give me a few minutes," Nate said. "I need to find Sam to cover the front desk." He left the bullpen as Lorenzo strode quickly toward Tate.

"What are you all looking at?"

Tate showed Lorenzo the photo and pointed to the guy in the background, skulking near the gazebo. "You know him?"

"This guy?" Lorenzo snorted. "Yeah."

Tate's interest perked at the derision in Lorenzo's voice. "How? Who is he?"

"I don't know his name. But about a month and

a half ago, I was at the park with my two youngest kids. You know Julie Waterman? Paul and Frannie's oldest? She's about to start her first year of college, I think."

Tate nodded. The Watermans had moved to Desparre long before he'd arrived, looking for a different lifestyle than they'd had back in Tulsa.

"Well, like most of the locals, she knows I'm a cop. She came over and told me this guy was creeping her out. Said he'd been watching her all afternoon."

Tate frowned. Was that why Sabrina hadn't gotten a note until recently? Because her stalker had been busy fixating on someone else for a while? It seemed odd that he'd track her all the way to Alaska and then get distracted, but maybe a month and a half ago, he'd known Sabrina was in Desparre but hadn't located her yet. Or maybe he was the kind of creep who always harassed women.

"So I went over to talk to him," Lorenzo continued. "I wasn't on duty, but I let him know I was a cop, tried to get his info. He acted like he didn't have ID on him and gave me a name I looked up later, but it was fake. Claimed he wasn't following anyone, but he was definitely aggravated. He left the park, but a few days later, I spotted him in his truck. I followed him just to see what he was up to, and he headed into the mountain. I lost him there, but I suspect he lives up that way."

"We need to find this guy, see how long he's been in town," Tate said. "See if he's ever lived in New York."

"You really think he's Sabrina's stalker?"

"Maybe. You see him watching Sabrina in this picture. She thinks he took a picture of her, too."

Lorenzo nodded, squinting at the picture again. "Could be he's just a garden-variety jerk and he comes to the park to stare at the women."

"Maybe," Tate agreed. "But he's the best lead we've got right now."

Tate was always careful not to get too excited about leads that could be coincidence because they could blind you to other options. But something about the way the guy was looking at Sabrina made all of Tate's protective instincts flare to life. His gut was telling him this was the guy.

Now they just needed to find him.

"Hey, Tate!" Nate said, rushing back into the room, wearing a big grin. "Guess what?"

Lorenzo smiled at his rookie partner, obviously amused at his enthusiasm.

"What?" Tate asked, a bad feeling forming that he couldn't explain.

"You and Sitka are famous."

The bad feeling turned into dread. "Why?"

Nate's brow furrowed. "What, you don't want to be famous? You're the only one. Anyway, the local story that Ariel Clemson wrote got picked up by national news!"

From what seemed like far away, Tate heard Lorenzo asking, "You okay, man?"

He couldn't seem to get it together enough to answer. Not only his first name but a picture of him was splashed across the national news.

He needed to drive home, take off his uniform and leave town now.

As the thought formed, his cell phone rang. He glanced at the screen. Keara.

No doubt she'd seen the story, too. There shouldn't be any hesitation now. He needed to go.

But he loved the life he'd built in Desparre. And even though the other officers were committed to Sabrina, he'd made her a promise. Besides, against all his instincts, he'd started to fall for her.

Tucking the phone back into his pocket and ignoring what he knew would be Keara's advice to run, Tate prayed the wrong people wouldn't see the story.

Because he needed to stay long enough to help Sabrina.

Chapter Eleven

It had been two days since the small heart-warming story Ariel Clemson had penned for the *Desparre Daily* had gone national. Two days without anyone showing up and trying to kill Tate. Two days without him receiving any death threats.

Maybe he'd gotten lucky.

The day after the story was picked up nationally, it was bumped out of the spotlight by a multistate manhunt for a group of escaped convicts. That story was still hogging the media's attention, enough so that Ariel approached him as he and Sitka walked downtown.

She had a pout firmly in place as she said, "I thought that story was going to be my big break."

"You'll get there," he assured her. He tried to appear sympathetic, though all he felt was relief that the story had been buried. Ariel didn't seem to notice that his concern was fake. She also didn't seem to notice that he couldn't stop his gaze from wandering away from her to study everyone around them. To see if he recognized someone from his past.

She shrugged and muttered, "I hope so," and then finally headed off, leaving him and Sitka alone.

With her gone, Tate gave in to his desire to

scan his surroundings again. The woods up ahead, where Sabrina's stalker might have disappeared after sending Talise's car racing toward Sitka, in particular kept grabbing his attention. Probably because of the way he'd been ambushed on a trail near the woods back in Boston.

Escaping that attempt on his life had been a result of his quick thinking and quick action. But it had also been partly luck. He couldn't help but wonder when his luck was going to run out.

In the news picture he was in the background, he reminded himself. Sabrina and Sitka had been the focus. Plus, the story didn't have his real last name. Even if Kevin and Paul were searching for him, how likely was it that they'd have set up alerts for just his first name? And he doubted they regularly read feel-good stories.

Still, as his cell phone rang yet again, it amped up Tate's anxiety even more. He felt guilty about not returning Keara's calls, but he didn't want to pick up while he was on patrol.

Sitka tilted her head, watching him as she strode alongside him. Her steady attention told him she knew something was wrong.

"It will all work out," he told her, hoping he was right. Every time he thought about leaving Desparre, the same no-win choice kept haunting him: Did he bring Sitka or did he leave her behind?

As if she could read his thoughts, she whined, high-pitched and sustained, until he pet her.

"I'm just trying to do the best thing for you," he said softly. Stroking her fur calmed his heart rate and seemed to relax her, too.

Ever since the incident with Talise's truck, he'd stopped using a leash with her in town. She didn't need one anyway, and if any locals had been wary of her before, Ariel's story seemed to have given them all a soft spot for their new police K-9.

Straightening, he headed for the park. He was hoping his luck would hold and he'd see the guy who Sabrina had identified in the photo, since it seemed he liked to hang out there. So far, police hadn't been able to positively identify him. Even quietly asking longtime locals hadn't yielded any results beyond "He looks familiar" or "He might live up the mountain" or "I think he moved here in the past couple of months."

When Tate reached the park, a group of kids ran over from the swings and started petting Sitka. His dog promptly sat, wagged her tail and tipped her head back, tongue lolling.

Tate held in a smile and resisted the urge to explain to the kids that he and Sitka were on duty. His dog was wearing her thick collar that identified her as a police K-9, but she wasn't wearing the dark vest that immediately screamed *Dog at Work*.

"How old is she?" one of the kids asked.

"Sitka is a year old," he told them. "She's an Alaskan Malamute. Did you know that this kind of dog got its start as an arctic sled dog?"

"Oh, cool," one of the other kids said.

"And feel her fur," he advised as Sitka's tail thumped harder, making the youngest of the kids laugh. "It's a double coat, and it's actually waterproof."

From the benches, several of their parents watched with amusement as Tate shared details about how Sitka worked as a police K-9.

"She can even find people who get lost," Tate continued, "by tracking them with her nose. It—"

Movement at the edge of his line of vision caught his attention, and Tate did a double take as he spotted the man from the picture, back behind the gazebo. When his gaze met Tate's, he slid his phone into his pocket and ran toward the street.

"Sitka, come on!" Tate called, as he pivoted and raced after the man.

Behind him, he could hear the parents calling their kids to get them out of Sitka's way.

Tate didn't wait for Sitka to break free of the kids. He just gritted his teeth and ran onto the street, determined not to let the guy escape.

Instead of taking a sharp turn into the woods as Tate had expected, the guy ran down a perpendicular street.

"Police!" Tate yelled after him. "Stop!"

The guy glanced back, giving Tate a better

look at a scowling, scared expression and a lot more muscle than had been evident in the photo. Since that picture had been taken, the guy had grown a short beard, as if he knew someone was looking for him.

Instead of heeding the directive, he ran even faster, and Tate swore at the speed such a muscle-bound guy should have had trouble achieving.

Yanking his radio off his duty belt, Tate panted, "I spotted the guy from the photo. He just took off on foot down Fleming Street. I'm in pursuit."

"Backup is on the way," Officer Sam Jennings returned immediately.

Behind him, the familiar sound of Sitka's footsteps were gaining, but Tate didn't slow to wait for her.

Ahead of him, the guy made a quick turn around the corner onto a street that housed nothing but a big, deserted warehouse. It was an eyesore in Desparre's otherwise nicely kept downtown, and it seemed like a strange spot to try and hide. Unless maybe he'd left a vehicle this way?

Tate pushed himself harder, pivoting onto the street fast.

He realized his mistake before he'd finished rounding the blind corner. But it was already too late.

The guy had stopped, hidden up against the massive warehouse. He stepped forward just as

Tate turned into view, lifted a huge, tattooed arm and clotheslined Tate.

Tate's feet went out from under him, and then he slammed into the dirt and pebbled ground. The impact stole his breath, and his vision went black.

Chapter Twelve

Tate fought his way out of the darkness, blinking his vision clear only to see the guy's massive fist heading toward his face.

Swallowing back nausea, Tate tried to roll out of the way.

Before he could, Sitka flew around the corner and leaped on the guy at a speed that dropped him to the ground.

As he flailed, yelled and swung those fists at Sitka's unprotected back, she bit down on his arm and shook her head.

He screamed louder and curled inward, then his feet rose like he was readying to kick her.

Shoving himself to a partly raised position, Tate pivoted and then knelt on top of the guy's legs, trapping them in place. "Let go, Sitka!" When Sitka dropped the guy's arm, Tate fought to flip him to his stomach.

The guy bucked and yanked an arm free, raising it to take a swing.

Then Sitka stepped closer and let out a deep growl.

The guy froze, panic in his suddenly wide eyes, and Tate didn't waste any time. He yanked the guy over until his face was pressed against the dirt road and wrenched his arms up behind him.

As Tate snapped on the cuffs, he asked, "Sitka, you okay?"

Woof!

It was part of her training to take down a suspect this way, but until now, she'd only done it in practice. At the training facility, the trainers, wearing protective gear, had shaken their arms and lifted her off the ground, teaching her to hang on through anything. They made loud noises next to her ears, lightly hit her back, and still she'd held tight.

Even though Tate had been proud of her, he'd hated seeing her get yanked around. Today had been worse. But judging by the tail wagging as she stood beside him, alert and ready to jump in again, she really was okay.

As his adrenaline calmed, Tate heard pounding feet heading toward them. "Back here!" he called.

"You good?" Officer Riera yelled back.

"All good!"

Lorenzo and Nate rounded the corner. The veteran was breathing hard as he leaned over and asked the guy, "You have anything on you that can stick me? Any needles or a knife?"

The guy on the ground forced his head to the side so he could look up at the five-foot-six Latino with muscles that rivaled his. He scowled, then shook his head.

"Rook?" Lorenzo used the nickname for the partner who hadn't been a true rookie in several months, since he'd marked a year on the force. "You want to check him?"

Lorenzo helped Tate pull the guy to his feet, and they watched as Nate patted him down. A minute later, he handed Tate a wallet and a cell phone.

Scowling at the guy who might have gotten his weapon if Sitka hadn't leaped in at the right moment, Tate opened the wallet and pulled out a driver's license. "Mario McKeever." His scowl deepened as he saw the state. "From New York."

"Let's get him processed," Lorenzo suggested, taking the guy by the crook of the arm as if he worried Tate would start an interrogation out in the street.

This was Sabrina's stalker. A good four inches shorter than Tate's six feet, with flexing biceps that suggested he spent a lot of time at the gym, he wore a snarl that made him look even more intimidating. His face wasn't all that memorable, with small features partly hidden by a thick layer of scruff. Still, now that Tate had a better view than the grainy picture they'd taken in the park, he knew for sure. He didn't recognize Mario from the social-media images he'd been poring over. How far on the outskirts of Sabrina's life had he been?

As Lorenzo and Tate led the suspect around the corner and toward the police station, with Nate and Sitka trailing slightly behind, Tate tried to keep his mouth shut. It was something he was good at; more than once, his old chief had asked him to stand in the room or help out with an interrogation of a challenging suspect because Tate wouldn't lose his cool.

But right now, thinking of the fear on Sabrina's face as she'd been trying to slip away at dawn, he couldn't help himself. "Why can't you just *leave her alone*?"

"Tate," Lorenzo warned.

Tate took a deep breath, then clamped his jaw shut.

Mario looked back and forth between them, then snapped, "I don't know what you're talking about, man. I ran because you and your attack dog started chasing me for no reason. You let me go now and I won't sue you. Look at my arm!"

He tried to pull it forward, but between the cuffs and Lorenzo's grip, he couldn't. He didn't need to move it for Tate to see the damage. Mario's forearm was bleeding, the bite wounds obvious.

Instead of telling him that Sitka wouldn't have knocked him down if he hadn't been a threat, Tate followed protocol this time and didn't engage. He managed to keep his silence all the way back to the station, where the new police chief was waiting.

"Let's get him fingerprinted," Chief Griffith said. Mario jerked back so quickly that Tate and the chief shared a look as Lorenzo yanked him forward again. The guy had a record.

"I need a doctor," Mario insisted, his eyes wide as he kept trying to pull away from Lorenzo.

"No problem," the chief said calmly. "We're going to get you some first aid right now, and then we'll take you to the hospital."

Tate ground his teeth together, trying to hold in his frustration. It was protocol. And with the guy in custody, Sabrina was out of danger. But he wanted more answers now—like how Mario had managed to track her all the way from New York.

The guy relaxed as another officer came in, snapped on a pair of gloves and wrapped up the wound. Then the chief took Mario's arm, pulling him farther into the station.

"What are you doing?" Mario demanded. "I've got rights! I want to see a doctor."

"And we're taking you to one," the chief replied. "But first we're going to have to get your prints."

Mario planted his feet, and his muscles bulged as he resisted the chief's tugs.

Showing a lot more calm than Tate felt, the chief just smiled and nodded at Officer Max Becker, who grinned and came over with the portable fingerprint system, pressing the suspect's thumb against it before he knew what was happening.

"Hey!" Mario yelled, yanking his hand away.

"Got it," Max said, backing away from Mario's swinging arms.

Mario's snarl returned, and every officer in the front of the station tensed at once, ready to react to an attack.

His gaze swept them, then he seemed to realize he was outmanned, and his head fell forward. The chief pulled him toward processing.

"Mario McKeever," Max announced. "We've got two stalking charges within the past decade. Resulted in a short stint in jail and a couple of restraining orders. And—" Max snorted as he looked back at Mario "—the reason he ran. He's wanted in a sexual-assault case back in New York."

"From when?" Tate asked.

"Four months ago."

"And then he came here," Tate said. "Lucky coincidence, or did he already know Sabrina was here?"

Mario twisted in the chief's grip. "I don't know a Sabrina. And I ran because I was framed."

He continued to protest as the chief frowned and called to Lorenzo. "Can you and Nate manage the hospital transport?"

"Sure," Lorenzo said, and the chief turned to Tate.

"Step outside with me."

As soon as they were out the door, Tate insisted, "I can go along. I'll be careful what I ask."

"Tate, it's not him," the chief said.

"What do you mean?"

"This isn't Sabrina's stalker."

"Come on," Tate insisted. "He was taking pictures of her. He's got a history of stalking. And he's from New York!"

"Coincidences, but not proof. This guy has a known stalking problem, and Sabrina isn't the only woman here he's taken pictures of." Before Tate could continue arguing, the chief said, "He's in the national database. He's wanted in New York. That means he would have popped for police in the murder of Dylan Westwood. But he didn't."

Tate swore under his breath. The chief was right. It was someone else's prints that had shown up in Sabrina's boyfriend's house. Someone without a record.

Was he wrong? Was Mario just a general creep and not specifically the creep harassing Sabrina?

What about the New York connection? He must have come here within the past few months—and then Sabrina's stalker had suddenly restarted contact. Was it all coincidence?

"Maybe Mario hired someone to make the hit on Westwood. Or maybe the murder wasn't actually committed by her stalker," Tate said. "Maybe he just capitalized on it, sent that note to Sabrina to make her think he had more power than he actually did."

The chief nodded slowly. "Yeah, both of those things are possible. We'll question Mario thoroughly. In the meantime, you and Sitka should take the rest of the day. Fill out your incident report and then head home. Take a break and get your head clear. We'll update you."

Tate shook his head, shocked that the chief thought he wasn't fit to be working. "Chief—"

"You're too invested. And while I'm not worried about you crossing a line, I also know Lorenzo and Nate can get the job done. I'll be watching the interrogation, too. But you were knocked to the ground today, and technically, you need to get checked out. I'll trust you to handle that. But I don't want you back on duty for twenty-four hours. Rest, have a doctor look at you, and I'll update you. Okay?"

Frowning, Tate nodded. It *was* protocol, especially since the world had gone black on him when he hit the ground. The chief didn't know that, but he was being cautious.

Even though Tate wanted to be the one questioning Mario, the closest hospital was one town over. That meant going up and down a mountain, an hour each way. And that didn't include time spent being checked out by a doctor.

That was time Tate could use to return to Sabrina's social media, see if he could find Mario McKeever somewhere on the platforms.

"Okay," he agreed.

The chief's eyes narrowed slightly at his ready agreement, but he didn't say anything as Tate opened the door to the station and called Sitka.

She came bounding out, and he led her to his personal vehicle. As he opened the door for her, she looked up at him questioningly, as if to ask *Why aren't we staying at work?*

"We have some things to do at home," he told her, as Lorenzo and Nate exited the police station and pulled Mario toward their police vehicle.

The criminal's eyes met his briefly, and then he scowled and looked away.

If this guy was Sabrina's stalker, Tate vowed to find the connection before Mario was back at the station for his interrogation.

But two hours later, as Tate checked the time yet again and Sitka whined at his feet, he had nothing. He'd been following every thread he could find from Sabrina's social media, through her brother, through friends and even friends of friends. He'd blown images up threefold, staring into the background, searching for Mario's unremarkable face or his nasty sneer.

How much time did he have left before Lorenzo and Nate brought Mario back to the station for questioning? Finding a link between Mario and Sabrina that they could show the suspect early in the process was likely to be far more effective than if they did it later, after he'd lawyered up and some of the initial shock of being caught had faded.

Rubbing a hand over his head, which was throbbing from two hours of staring at his computer screen and the bump to the back of his head earlier, Tate clicked back to one of Sabrina's friends who posted the most publicly available pictures. She and Sabrina didn't appear to be especially close, but he'd found Sabrina in the background of several of her older pictures. Maybe he needed to go back even further. Maybe Mario had fixated on her long before he'd started writing to her.

He opened a photo from three years ago on the woman's feed and found Sabrina, laughing in the background. The lighting was crap, the surroundings some dimly lit bar. She was surrounded by a couple of people he recognized from hours of looking through feeds as work colleagues. Beyond that were more people who seemed to be part of the same crowd.

His shoulders dropped. It had seemed like a real long shot, but he was still disappointed that none of them were Mario McKeever.

Then his pulse shot up, and he leaned in close to the screen as a familiar face in the background caught his attention.

Beside him, Sitka got to her feet, whining as she caught his mood.

"No way," he muttered, blowing the picture

up. It got grainier as the size increased, but he wasn't wrong. The guy standing two rows behind Sabrina—maybe part of the group, maybe not— had his gaze solidly fixed on her.

It wasn't Mario McKeever. It was worse.

It was a man Sabrina trusted, one of the few people in Desparre she seemed to consider a friend. It was a man who'd been in the forefront of the photo in the park with Mario. He'd been talking to Sabrina, completely overlooked as a threat because he'd supposedly moved here after his wife had died.

It was Adam Lassiter.

Chapter Thirteen

"Adam." Sabrina heard the surprise in her own voice as she opened the door to her cabin.

Her friend was standing on the front stoop slightly hunched forward, hands shoved in his pockets. "Hey, Sabrina. I'm sorry to stop by unannounced, but I…" He blew out a breath, then gave a self-conscious smile. "I just needed a friend, and since you lived kind of nearby…"

Sabrina glanced around at the vast expanse of woods surrounding her cabin, the enclosure that had felt like a protective barrier when she'd first arrived. Now it felt like a place for a stalker to hide. Even standing in her open doorway felt too exposed.

She hadn't invited anyone except Tate and Sitka inside in two long years. Adam might be her friend, but the idea of letting anyone too close still made anxiety knot her stomach.

"I should have called," Adam said, stepping back. "It's just—I didn't have your number. But Lora told me where you lived, and I was passing near here, so I thought maybe… I'm sorry."

Her gaze snapped back up to him. They didn't really have the sort of friendship where you just showed up unannounced. She wasn't even sure how Lora had known where she lived to be able to tell him, but it didn't really surprise her that she knew it. Lora seemed to know everything about everyone.

As her attention refocused on Adam instead of the vast expanses where someone could be hiding behind him, she realized he looked worse than usual. There were deep circles under his eyes, as if he hadn't been sleeping. A downward tilt to his mouth as if he'd been frowning all day.

"I'm sorry," she told Adam, trying to shake off her unease. She almost hadn't opened the door, even after seeing through the peephole that it was just him. "It's been a tough week."

"For me, too." His words were soft as his gaze lifted from the ground back up to her. "Today would have been my wife's birthday." He took another step backward, shaking his head, his back and shoulders sloped inward. "I was going to go for a walk, clear my head. And then I realized I didn't want to be all alone. But it's an imposition. I'm sorry. I—"

"No," Sabrina cut him off as guilt bubbled up that she'd made him feel like he couldn't reach out to her.

In the few months she'd tried to venture out more, Adam and Lora had made her feel like she could have friends here. Even if she couldn't tell them the truth about who she was, she'd always thought Adam had sensed she'd also experienced a recent loss. It was in the way his gaze sometimes cut to her when he mentioned his grief, as if he expected her to share her own loss.

She never had. She'd been tempted once or twice to talk about it, to be vague enough that she wouldn't get tripped up on her real past. But something had always stopped her, a voice in the back of her head that sounded like the PI saying not to take any risks she might regret. Not to give in to the desire for connection at the expense of safety.

So right now, instead of inviting him inside, she grabbed her keys off the table in her entryway and stepped outside. Her fingers fluttered briefly up to the emergency button hidden underneath her T-shirt as she locked the door behind her. Then she mustered up a smile and said, "Lead the way."

An answering smile trembled on his face, but it didn't quite reach his eyes. "Thanks."

He walked down her drive, out to the dirt road. Then, instead of heading toward town, he moved in the other direction, where the woods started slowly thinning out as the road tilted upward. "There's a great view about a mile from here. A good place to clear your head," he said, keeping a brisk pace.

He was about four inches taller than her and Sabrina had to increase her pace to keep up with his long strides. She struggled with the appropriate thing to say, but words evaded her. She had no idea how his wife had passed, but she was pretty sure he was only a few years older than her, in his early to midthirties. Young to have lost a spouse.

He was probably here because he thought she knew that same kind of grief. But although the horror of Dylan's death would probably always be with her, it was different. They'd only been dating for three months before he was murdered. It had been the beginning of something, but where it would lead she'd never know. She couldn't begin to guess the grief he was experiencing.

He kept hurrying along, slightly ahead of her, and unease pricked as he moved off the road and onto a path with a steeper incline. Her thoughts went immediately to the bear and cubs Tate and Sitka had run into behind her house.

"Adam?" she huffed. She'd been in good shape back in New York, often choosing a long walk instead of public transportation. But since going into hiding, she'd been afraid to go running alone. She always felt safer behind the locked door of a vehicle or a hotel room.

He glanced back at her, slowing slightly. "Sorry. I hike a lot."

"No, it's not that. There are bears in the woods."

He laughed, although it sounded a little forced. "Nah. I've come this way plenty of times. We'll be fine. Trust me, the view will be worth it. You wouldn't think so, but there's a big drop-off this way. It's an amazing place to look out onto the valley below. You just can't get too close to the edge." He laughed again, a little chortle that sounded like he was trying too hard to be cheerful for her sake. "And anyway, I have bear spray." He patted the pocket of his cargo pants as he kept moving up the path.

Sabrina hesitated, glancing back down the empty road, then into the forest. The trees were thinner here than by her house, but that didn't mean it wasn't a great place for bears to wander.

Up ahead, Adam was still pressing forward, not realizing she wasn't right behind him. Since they'd left her house, he hadn't said a word about his wife. Maybe he'd just needed silent, understanding company. Or maybe he wanted to wait until they reached this peaceful view he'd mentioned. But something about the way he'd shown up and then just plowed forward was making discomfort creep in.

Was she being paranoid? Adam was her friend. One of her only friends.

But she'd learned a long time ago that her stalker wasn't the only threat. That sometimes, danger came in the guise of a friend. Like the coworker who'd walked her out to her car, joking about women sticking together, then nodded at someone hiding in the shadows. That guy had rushed for her, only charging the other way when one of the cooks happened to pop open the back door for a smoke. She'd left that place behind like so many others, but she thought she'd carried the lesson with her.

Sabrina's hand reached for the alert button without conscious intent.

Then, Adam glanced back and called, "Come on!"

At some point, she had to be able to trust her own judgment again. At some point, her life couldn't be all about fear.

She lowered her hand, hurrying to catch up.

Yes, her stalker was here. But so was Tate, who'd dedicated himself to helping her, who represented a possibility even greater. So were Adam and Lora, people who'd befriended her despite how closed off she was. Who'd given her a chance when they could have walked away. Maybe she needed to do the same.

The path Adam had chosen was thin, not enough room for them to walk side by side even if she could keep up with his pace. The edges of wispy pine trees brushed her arms as she alternated between walking and a semijog. Her breath came in uneven puffs that reminded her how long it had been since she'd felt comfortable going anywhere. The reminder made anger knot in her chest, but it also made the view that appeared as they crested the hill more spectacular.

Adam was right. It was like the forest suddenly dropped away. Way down below was a green valley, spotted with trees. In the middle, she could see a group of animals.

Stepping up beside him at the edge, she glanced briefly his way, feeling a smile break free. An image of his expression, strangely pensive, flickered in the edge of her vision as she moved a little closer to the edge, straining to see. "Moose?"

"Yeah."

His voice was closer than she'd expected, and as she twisted toward him in surprise, she felt something shove against her back, right under her shoulder blade.

Her arms jolted up, a desperate attempt at regaining her balance as her stomach dropped and the valley below seemed to reach up toward her.

Then Adam's arm clamped around her biceps, and he yanked her backward.

Breathing hard, Sabrina stared at him, then glanced behind her. Had she imagined a push? Had something fallen from a tree?

Her arm twitched under his grasp, fear squirming in her belly.

Letting go, Adam stepped slightly away. "Sorry. Did I scare you? You looked like you were slipping. I didn't mean to grab you so hard. I thought you were going to fall."

"No, that's—" The spot beneath her shoulder blade prickled with the feel of that phantom force. Had she imagined it? Had she just slipped?

She glanced down at the loose pebbles where she'd been standing, then back up at Adam.

There was something different in his eyes, hurt that she'd misinterpreted his help. Before she could say anything, he took another step backward.

"Maybe we should head back," he suggested. He didn't wait for her to answer, just moved away from her, down the path.

With one last glance around, Sabrina hurried after him.

Chapter Fourteen

"Sabrina, damn it, call me back!"

Tate hung up the phone and grabbed his keys. "Come on, Sitka."

She leaped to her feet, tail wagging as she chased him down the stairs and out to the truck.

His mood was decidedly less jolly, a dread in his gut that no amount of telling himself he was overreacting would calm. He'd called Sabrina three times in a row before leaving a voice mail. He had no idea how close she kept her cell phone. Maybe she was in the shower, perfectly fine but unable to hear the ringing. Or maybe she was in town, chatting away with Talise in the grocery store, her phone tucked in her pocket, ringing unheard underneath Talise's nonstop stories.

"Let's just check," he muttered, opening the door for Sitka, then hopping up into the cab beside her. Then they were taking a route that had become familiar over the past week, out to Sabrina's cabin.

As he drove, his gaze swept the narrow road, bracketed by beautiful old trees, seeing it all in a new way. Sabrina's cabin was too isolated. Even with an alert button connecting her directly to the police, he'd seen firsthand what the vast distances out here could mean when responding to an emergency call.

He clenched the wheel tighter, pressing down on the gas as Sitka hunched low in the passenger seat. He should have insisted that Sabrina move into town and stay at the hotel until they'd found her stalker. Better yet, he should have offered her his pullout couch and convinced his colleagues to trade off shifts at his house watching her.

It was impractical. Impossible to sustain. But right now, knowing that Adam Lassiter had once lived in New York City, had once been photographed staring at Sabrina from afar, made panic and guilt tense his entire body.

They'd known he was close. They'd known he was escalating.

But they'd never suspected it was someone Sabrina trusted, someone she called a friend. What if they'd miscalculated how much time they had to stop him before Sabrina paid the price?

Sitka whined, catching his anxiety, and Tate gave her a quick pet meant to reassure. She just whined again, softer, as she hunched lower on the seat.

When he finally pulled up to the cabin, he released a deep, relieved breath. Sabrina's car was in the drive. She was home. Even though he'd gotten the impression she'd never let anyone inside besides him, he was happy not to see any other vehicle in the drive.

Parking behind her, he stepped out, then turned back to whistle for Sitka.

She was already leaping out of the truck and bounding toward the front door.

Tate slammed the truck door and hurried after her. Then he knocked on Sabrina's door loudly, calling out, "Sabrina? It's Tate. Are you home? I need to talk to you."

There was no answer.

Unease settled in his chest, and his hand dropped automatically to where he normally kept his duty belt and his weapon. But he'd run out of the house so quickly, he hadn't even thought about snapping it back on.

Stepping off the porch, he followed the same path along the side of her house that Sitka had taken when she'd tracked a scent. Instead of moving into the woods, he crept along the edge of Sabrina's house.

Sitka kept pace with him. Her nose nudged his leg hard every few steps, like she was demanding an answer about what they were doing.

"We're looking for Sabrina," he told her softly. If someone was inside with her, preventing her from answering, they'd know Tate was here. But he didn't want to advertise his location.

He was probably being paranoid, and she was simply wearing headphones or had a dead battery in her cell phone. But he couldn't take any chances.

Knowing how safety-conscious she was, he didn't expect to find an open window, but he hoped to at least find one that would give him a view inside. The curtains were all down, but on the far side of the cabin, he discovered one of the windows was old. It would be easy to pop the lock.

If she was inside dancing around the cabin with music blasting in a pair of headphones, he'd apologize profusely and replace the window. If not… Gritting his teeth, Tate wrenched the window upward and sideways at the same time, and it slipped free of the old locking mechanism.

Pushing it open, he moved the curtain aside and peered into a bathroom. "Stay," he told Sitka as he hauled himself inside. If he needed her, she could leap through that window easily.

He landed awkwardly on the other side, with a lot more noise than he'd hoped to make. Pushing himself to a partially upright position, he peered around the corner. Seeing no one, he eased into the connected bedroom.

It looked like the rest of the cabin, with functional, comfortable furniture. There wasn't a lot of Sabrina's personality on display, except for a pile of colorful drawings pinned to the wall above the dresser and pictures of her mom and brother on the side table.

Moving forward, he did a slow and careful check of the second bedroom, then moved into the open kitchen and living area. She wasn't here.

Confusion turned quickly into dread as he saw

her phone on the kitchen table. Tapping the button to check that it wasn't dead, he saw notifications of all his missed calls, but nothing else evident without unlocking it.

Why was her car here if she wasn't? He couldn't imagine her walking into town, but where else would she go? Still, if she was in trouble, why was there no sign of a struggle and no alert from her emergency button?

Grabbing Sabrina's sweatshirt from where it lay draped over the couch, Tate hurried to the front door and let himself outside. Sitka was standing beside him before he'd closed the door behind him. "Time to track," he told her.

Her tail wagged as he held out Sabrina's shirt and let her sniff it. Then her nose dropped to the ground, and she pivoted toward the driveway.

Tate felt a hint of relief as she led him down the drive instead of into the woods, but it faded just as fast. Where had she gone? And had she gone alone?

When Sitka turned right instead of left at the end of the drive, heading away from downtown instead of toward it, his anxiety increased. Then his dog let out a happy bark and started running.

Tate's gaze jolted to the right, where Sabrina was emerging from the woods far down the road. Stifling a curse of equal parts frustration and relief, Tate ran after Sitka.

"Sitka," Sabrina exclaimed, jogging until she

met his dog in the middle of the road. She knelt in front of Sitka, wrapping her arms around the dog's neck in a brief hug that told Tate something had spooked her.

Tate skidded to a stop beside them, scanning the woods as his heart thudded too fast and anger knotted in his chest at how overemotional he'd gotten. He'd been so worried that he'd left his weapon behind. Now how much of a barrier would he be against a threat?

"What's going on?" He wrapped his arm around Sabrina's upper arm, pulling her upright.

She flinched, pulling her arm free and rubbing it.

His gaze met hers, even more troubled because he hadn't grabbed her *that* hard. "What are you doing wandering around the woods alone? I've been calling you."

"I—I'm sorry. I went for a walk with Adam and—"

"Adam?" His pulse skyrocketed as he scanned the woods again. He didn't see the man anywhere. Had Sabrina managed to escape from him? Or had they gotten lucky and Adam had just been trying to see how close he could get to Sabrina?

Or was Tate wrong entirely, and it was merely a bizarre coincidence? He'd learned in past cases that you couldn't get too focused on one suspect at the expense of others. Mario McKeever might not have killed Sabrina's boyfriend himself, but that didn't mean he hadn't hired someone to do it. It didn't mean he hadn't been stalking her and simply taken advantage of someone else's crime to scare her.

Sabrina crossed her arms over her chest, and she glanced around the woods, shivering. "What's going on?"

Obviously sensing her distress, Sitka leaned against her. His dog didn't always recognize her own size, and she must have leaned hard, because Sabrina stumbled slightly before dropping her arms and absently petting Sitka.

"Where is Adam now?"

Sabrina shook her head, gesturing vaguely behind her. "I don't know. I wanted to come back, and he said he wanted to keep walking. He turned back into the woods when we got close to the road, and I kept going."

Tate lowered his voice. "So he could be nearby?" Not waiting for Sabrina's answer, he put his hand on her back, ushering her forward. "Let's go to your place. Now."

"Tate, what—"

"*Now*, Sabrina."

She started to run, and Tate gave Sitka a nod. His dog raced up beside her, and Tate followed slightly behind, his gaze pivoting all around, even though he knew most likely if Adam was still around, he was behind them.

His heart didn't stop racing until they were

back in Sabrina's house and he'd checked all
the rooms again, locked the door and braced the
wooden handle of her mop in the bathroom window. Then he called the station and gave them an
update, requesting backup and an extra weapon.

After hanging up, he met Sabrina in the living room. She stood in the center of the room,
anxiety on her face as she stroked Sitka's head.

"What's happening?" she whispered.

"What did Adam say when he showed up?"
Tate demanded. "You took his car out to the
woods? Where did he leave it?"

"I…" She frowned, shook her head. "He said
it would have been his wife's birthday. She died
a few months ago. He wanted company. He said
there was a great view out in the woods, and he
was right. It was beautiful. We went for a walk.
He—"

"You went for a walk? What about his vehicle?"

"I—I don't know. I guess I didn't think about
it when he showed up, but I didn't see a vehicle.
Maybe he walked here? He said he lived nearby.
Or…" She frowned again. "Maybe he said he hap-
pened to be nearby. He said Lora told him where
I lived, and he just didn't want to be alone today."

"And then what?" Tate asked, knowing his
rapid-fire questions without answers were making her more nervous. But none of this made
much sense. If Adam had gotten Sabrina alone,

why hadn't he made a move to grab her? If his goal was to harm her, why not now? Or maybe he'd come to Alaska, realized he could start over as her friend and woo her long-term, with her never being the wiser that he'd once stalked her and killed her boyfriend.

"Then I followed him up that road awhile, and into the woods. He took me to this beautiful drop-off and…" Her lips twisted, her forehead creasing with confusion. "I'm not sure what happened. I thought someone pushed me, but then Adam grabbed me and kept me from falling. I looked down, and there were a lot of loose rocks, so maybe I just slipped? Or something fell from a tree?"

"Or Adam pushed you, then saved you," Tate said grimly.

"Why would he do that?" Sabrina demanded, crossing her arms over her chest again. She seemed to fold inward, visibly shrinking as Sitka whined, glancing back and forth between them.

"I found him in a picture with you that one of your coworkers took back in New York. I think he might be your stalker."

"But—" fear mingled with the confusion on Sabrina's face "—he's new to Desparre, and he's always lived in Alaska. His wife died a few months ago. He—"

"How do you know that's true?" Tate asked.

"I… I guess I don't. But Lora told me a lot of

it. She introduced me. She's known Adam longer than I have. She's the one who told him where I lived."

"Okay." Tate nodded. "You have Lora's number?"

"Yeah." Sabrina spun and grabbed her phone off the kitchen table. She paused, her gaze darting back to him, probably as she noticed all his missed calls. Then she tapped her phone and handed it to him.

She had Lora's number pulled up. He hit Send and waited only briefly before Lora answered cheerfully, "Sabrina! How are you?"

"This is Officer Tate Emory. I—"

"Oh, no! Is Sabrina okay?"

"Yes. I'm sorry, Lora. She's fine. Look, I need to ask you some things in confidence, okay?" When she hesitantly agreed, he asked, "How long have you known Adam Lassiter?"

"Adam?" There was surprise in her voice. "Um, I guess about three months, since he moved here."

"Where did he move from? Did you know his late wife? Or have you seen pictures of her?"

"He lived in Fairbanks most of his life. He said his wife died about a month before he moved to Desparre. He wanted to get away from the constant reminders of her. I'm sorry, but what's going on? Why do you want to know about Adam?"

"What did he say when he asked for Sabrina's address?"

"He never asked me for Sabrina's address. I don't even know where she lives."

A curse lodged in Tate's throat as his own phone rang. "Lora, I'll get back to you, okay? But keep this conversation between us. And one more thing. Do you know where Adam lives?"

"Kind of. If you take the main road out of town north for a while, he's in the woods. A little cabin. I don't know the exact location."

The dread building in his gut amplified. "Thanks, Lora."

"Why did she tell him my address?" Sabrina asked as Tate hung up her phone and answered his own.

"She didn't," Tate told her. "But Adam lives somewhere out this way." Lifting his phone to his ear, Tate said, "Emory. What's going on?"

"We're coming up on Sabrina's place," Charlie Quinn answered. "You'll hear us in two minutes."

"Thanks. We also need to get someone on finding Adam's address. According to one of Sabrina's friends, he lives out this way somewhere."

"Yeah, that's my other update," Charlie said, his tone telling Tate before he finished speaking that it wasn't good news. "We can't find any information on an Adam Lassiter who fits his description. Not in Desparre and, as far as Max could tell with a quick search, not in Alaska."

Tate's gaze darted to Sabrina, who was watching him wide-eyed and wary. "It's not his real name."

"Probably not," Charlie agreed. "And without his real name…"

Charlie didn't continue, but he didn't have to. If Adam got any hint that police were here, if he'd been watching from the woods as Tate ran up to Sabrina, Adam might hide.

Without a real name, how would they be able to track him?

Chapter Fifteen

Two hours later, Sabrina sat at Tate's desk in the bullpen of the Desparre police station. Blown up to two hundred percent on the computer screen in front of her was a picture taken by a coworker back in New York almost three years ago. A good three months before she'd received the first letter from her stalker.

In the picture, she was smiling and laughing. She wanted to reach out and touch the screen, try to recapture that level of happiness. There was no cloud of fear hanging over her then, no paranoia. Three years wasn't that long ago, and yet, that feeling seemed so out of reach now.

Behind her, maybe loosely a part of the group she was with, maybe not, was someone who sure looked like Adam Lassiter. The picture was grainy enough that she couldn't be positive. If it was really Adam, he'd lost about fifty pounds, replacing it with lean muscle. He'd also cut his hair close to the scalp, making it seem lighter than it did in the photo. He even dressed differently now, in a lot of cargo pants and T-shirts, rather than the striped button-down from the photo.

Maybe it was just wishful thinking to believe it might not be the same person. She'd talked to Adam, laughed with Adam. She'd walked blithely into the woods with him alone. She'd almost invited him into her house.

All her earlier feelings of determination to move forward, to trust her own judgment again and stop jumping at shadows, fell away. What was left was a sadness that seemed to hollow her out.

Tate's hand closed over her forearm, and when she glanced at him, there was sympathy in his gaze.

She eased her arm away and turned to face him. The other officers were occupied on their computers trying to dig up more information about Adam, yet she kept her voice soft, so much so that he leaned closer. Ever since they'd gotten to the station, she'd been holding in her question about how he'd found Adam in an old picture. There was only one way she could imagine. "How did you figure out my last name?"

Guilt crossed over his face, quickly enough that she wasn't sure if she'd imagined it. "I looked for information on a murder in New York City from two years ago where news stories mentioned a stalker."

She nodded and turned back to the computer, saying nothing. The most basic information about why she was running, and it had given away more details about herself than she'd wanted to share.

"I'm sorry," he said, maneuvering so he was in her line of sight, as Sitka whined at her side.

She didn't respond to either of them, just continued to stare at the image. How had she been so wrong? "Do you think Adam was trying to push me off that cliff? Then he changed his mind and grabbed me?"

"I doubt it," Tate said, but his tone told her what he thought was worse.

Reluctantly, she refocused her gaze on him.

"I think both were intentional from the start. He gave you a push *so* he could save you. Create a sense of obligation, make you feel grateful to him. More trusting."

She snorted, not quite meeting Tate's gaze. "It didn't work. I thought I'd offended him, which I figured was why he wanted to keep going on his own."

Tate nodded. "Maybe that's what happened. His plan backfired, and he decided to continue playing the long game."

Her hands tightened into fists, and she knew her anger wasn't all about Adam. Yes, Tate digging into her background had probably found her stalker. But he'd still betrayed her trust. "It's not a game. It's my *life*."

Tate took hold of the arms of her chair and turned her to face him. He knelt in front of her, and Sitka scooted over, forcing her head onto his knee, her puppy eyes staring up at Sabrina.

The expression on Sitka's face threatened to soften her. Before Tate could speak, she said, "I understand why you dug up information on me. It worked, so I guess I have no right to be mad. But—"

"You have every right to be mad," Tate said. "I should have told you. You've given up so many pieces of your identity to try to feel safe, and I broke your trust. That's another way to make you feel unsafe, and I'm sorry."

Lifting her gaze to his, she saw sincerity, even regret, in his eyes. How had he known exactly what she was feeling? He spoke as if he really did understand. But it was more than that. She'd chosen to trust him in a way she hadn't trusted anyone else in a long time. And he'd still gone behind her back.

She'd been by herself for two years. But she'd never felt more alone than she did right now.

Tate cringed, as if he could read her thoughts. Then he fit his hand around hers and whispered, "I really am sorry, Sabrina. You're... I care about you. All I want to do is help you."

She glanced from his hand, which felt so comforting on hers, even though he was part of the reason she hurt right now. She wished they were anywhere but at the police station, with his chief watching across the room. Pulling her hand free, she scooted her chair slightly backward, away from him.

Sitka let out another low whine, and Sabrina forced a lightness to her voice she didn't feel.

"It's okay, Sitka." She pet the dog until her tail thumped, then told Tate, "I forgive you. Let's figure out…"

She trailed off as the image of Adam caught the corner of her eye. Seeing it from this angle sparked a memory, brought the image she hadn't really remembered into focus. She'd been out for a coworker's birthday, at a bar that was too loud. The bar had been stuffy, the night too hot, the drinks flowing too freely. After a few hours, she'd started to feel more comfortable, have more fun.

The woman in the forefront of the picture with her—Jessamyn, who'd later become a good friend—had sensed her discomfort, grabbed her arm and taken her around the bar, introducing her to everyone, even people Jessamyn didn't know. And a group of guys who were friends of one of Jessamyn's friends.

"I think I remember him," she breathed, as more of the evening solidified in her mind.

Each of the guys had given their names, and some of them had provided other random information about themselves, like their job or hobbies. Her gaze had floated over each of them quickly. She remembered laughing through most of the introductions, partly because she'd been a little tipsy and partly because she'd been having fun.

She hadn't spoken to Adam again that night, that much she was sure. After being introduced to the group, she'd set down her beer and gotten onto the dance floor with Jessamyn. She hadn't left it until a few hours later, when she'd hopped into a cab and gone home.

"What do you remember?" Tate asked, making her refocus on him.

She let out an ironic laugh. "Periphery of my life is no joke. The most conversation we had was a quick introduction. I told him my name, he said his, and I was off to the dance floor. I never saw him again."

"Are you sure?"

"Pretty sure."

Tate nodded. "I don't suppose you remember his name?"

"You really don't think it's Adam Lassiter?"

"Well, we haven't found any property in his name, nor have we found any Adam Lassiter that matches his description. So, I'm thinking it's not his real name."

"I don't remember. All those guys were a blur, just a quick hello and on to the next person. It was a party. I was new to my job and made friends with coworkers that night. That's mostly what I remember."

"It's okay," Tate told her. "We'll dig it up."

"Tate."

Sabrina looked up, and Tate stood as the chief reached his desk.

"Chief. What is it?"

Chief Griffith nodded at her. "Sabrina." Then

he looked at them both as he said, "I spoke to your friend Lora. We asked her to call Adam, but he's not answering."

"He should show up in town eventually, though, right?" Sabrina asked. Or had he been close behind her when she'd trekked back toward the road and discovered Tate and Sitka waiting for her? Had he realized his identity was blown and already disappeared?

The way the chief's lips tightened made dread settle in her stomach even before he replied. "When you were giving me a rundown of what happened with Adam in the woods, Officer Emory here was drawing a map for two of our other officers. He detailed exactly where Sitka went through the woods when she was tracking from your house last week."

"Did they find anything?"

The chief glanced at Tate again, and something unspoken seemed to pass between them, something that made Tate's expression tighten, too. "We found a cabin. It's old, and the bank foreclosed on it last year when the guy who owned it passed away. It's been sitting empty ever since, at least as far as anyone knew."

"Adam was squatting there?" Tate asked, fury on his face. "Where is this place?"

The chief nodded. "We think so. We found evidence that someone has been there recently, including some clothes, food and pinholes in the wall like something had been posted there. It looks like it was cleared out in a hurry."

Tate swore as the chief fixed his attention entirely on her.

Sabrina stiffened as he continued. "This cabin would take a while to get to on the road from your place, but if you go directly through the woods, it's about a mile away, a straight shot. You probably never even knew anyone was back there."

The dread intensified, a familiar feeling from her early days of running, constantly feeling like her stalker was right behind her. She thought it had just been paranoia, but had he been there all along?

SIX DAYS AFTER Adam had cleared out of the cabin behind hers, there was no sign of him.

Sabrina had spent the time alternating between extreme emotions. One day, she'd be certain a police officer would knock on the door to the hotel room where they'd stuck her and announce that it was all over and she could go home to the family she hadn't dared to contact in two years. The next day, she'd be sure this would continue forever and she'd be forced to make a new impossible choice: go back to running and assume Adam was right behind her in every new town or stay here and wait for the police to run out of resources to waste on her. Wait for him to come after her.

Most likely the story Adam had told about living in Alaska all his life, about having recently lost a wife, were all lies to make her feel comfortable letting him get close. It had been brilliant. Especially befriending Lora before he'd ever approached her. Getting the story secondhand that he was a widower mourning the too-recent loss of his wife had immediately ruled him out in her mind as her stalker.

The fact that he'd appeared in a picture with her in New York suggested he'd actually lived there, at least for some amount of time. If he'd grown up in the city like her, there had to be only so long he could hide out in the treacherous Alaskan wilderness before the locals tracked him down.

But they hadn't found him yet.

Meanwhile, she was going stir-crazy in the ridiculously opulent room in Desparre's only hotel, the luxury Royal Desparre. When she'd nervously asked about the cost, Tate had said it was being taken care of and insisted it was safer than being in the middle of nowhere. She still had her alert button and the owners—who doubled as management—knew to call the police if they spotted Adam. Tate checked in several times a day, usually by phone, but he and Sitka also stopped by every night.

Still, she spent most of her days alone. Since she couldn't contact anyone and there were only so many hours she could spend making jewelry, especially with her creativity having taken a dive, she was bored. Having too many hours to think was making her more anxious.

So, when there was a knock on her door, she was up and reaching for the lock before her mind caught up and she checked the peephole. A grin burst free, and a familiar anticipation settled in her stomach when she saw Tate standing on the other side, looking serious in his uniform but holding a pizza box.

He didn't usually finish up at the station and make his way over to her hotel until almost eight, so she'd gotten used to waiting for dinner. They'd never made plans to eat together each night, but he kept showing up until it felt like a standing date. Only the fact that he wore his uniform and always updated her on their progress reminded her each day that it wasn't really a date. Reminded her that nothing she felt for Tate could be permanent.

She still hadn't fully forgiven him for digging into her past without her permission, for not telling her when he'd learned her real name and searched her brother's social media. But he'd done it to help her. And it had worked. The more time she spent with him, the less she wanted to think about the mistakes in the past. The more she wanted to entertain a future that somehow had him in it.

It wasn't meant to be. But she could pretend.

Flinging open the door, she asked, "How did you know I needed some pizza?"

Woof! Sitka walked forward, butting Sabrina hard enough with her nose to knock her back a step.

As Tate reminded his dog to relax, Sabrina laughed and leaned down to pet her. "I think she wants pizza, too."

Woof!

Grinning, Tate followed his dog into the room, closing and locking the door behind him like always.

Sabrina couldn't help the flutter of nerves that erupted in her stomach. They seemed to be increasing in intensity each evening she spent with him. Since updates on the case only took so long—especially since there'd been nothing to report on Adam, and the guy they'd arrested last week still wasn't talking—their conversations had been getting more personal.

He'd already dug through her life on his own, so she'd decided she might as well tell him the truth about everything. The decision had been freeing.

And, she had to admit as he set the pizza box on the table by the window, the man looked good in his dark blue police uniform. She'd been attracted to him from the start, admired the thick dark brows that added even more intensity to his angular face and fixated on the full lips that drew her attention. But she'd always found that she grew more physically attracted to a man when she was emotionally attracted to him, too. Every day she spent with Tate, that attraction increased.

He turned back toward her, and from the way he went still, she knew her feelings were broadcasted across her face.

Ducking her head on the pretext of petting Sitka, Sabrina cursed her pale skin, which felt like it was on fire.

When she finally had her blush under control, she lifted her head again and found that Tate had crossed the room without her hearing him.

With Sitka sitting between them, he stood in front of her, his gaze locked on hers, a matching desire in his deep brown eyes.

She swayed forward, leaning over Sitka, without even consciously planning to do it.

He leaned toward her, captured her hands in his, and the touch sent sparks over her skin and up her arms.

Her lips tingled in anticipation, and as she moistened them with her tongue, his gaze darted there.

His voice sounded slightly strangled as he told her, "I have news."

News? Her brain struggled to focus on anything other than the heat in his eyes and the closeness of his lips. "About the investigation?"

"Yeah."

She stared at him, trying to decide what to pursue, until he finally gave her a half grin and leaned slightly away.

He kept hold of her hands, though, his fingers stroking lightly against her knuckles a distraction. "Mario McKeever still isn't talking. But we've been able to confirm his whereabouts two years ago. He's from New York, but he hasn't lived there in almost four years. And when you were getting notes, he was living in South Carolina and having regular run-ins with the law. No arrests, but the local police definitely knew his name."

"Okay," she said, her brain still processing everything more slowly. But she didn't want to pull her hands away, break the connection he'd initiated. "We were already pretty sure it was Adam, so that's not much news, right?"

"No. But I thought you'd want to know." He paused again, and she could see the fight in his eyes as his gaze drifted back to her lips. "There is one other thing. Since it's been almost a week with no sign of Adam, Chief Griffith suggested a plan to lure him back into the open. Stop waiting on his timetable and take back some control."

"Okay." Now, this was an idea Sabrina could get behind. She was tempted to lick her lips again, just to see if it would break Tate's concentration, but she resisted as his gaze lifted back to hers.

"Adam's MO has been to go after anyone who

might be a source of support, right? I mean, he came after me and Sitka after presumably seeing me stop by your house. And of course, there's Dylan."

Sabrina nodded, the memory of the police showing up at Dylan's family's lake house with the news of his death erasing all desire. "Yes."

"So, the chief thinks we should use that to our advantage. Get him angry enough to come after someone again."

Sabrina frowned at him. "Who? How? I don't want to put anyone at risk. I don't really have any friends here except Lora and—"

"You have me," Tate said, his tone firm. "We're going to make sure Adam takes the bait so we can take him down. The chief doesn't want it to look like I'm a friend, a source of support. He wants us to publicly play out a romance and get Adam to take his shot."

Chapter Sixteen

Tate held Sabrina's hand loosely in his own as he walked in downtown Desparre. Her long delicate fingers, slightly calloused from making jewelry, felt so right in his. There was a smile on his face he didn't need to fake or force, but it didn't mean he'd lost sight of the dangers.

The bench straight ahead, still crumpled and destroyed from the truck Sabrina's stalker might have sent after Sitka, was a stark reminder. So were the woods beyond that, which looked too much like the forest in Boston he'd darted into to escape his fellow officers' gunfire.

The desire to constantly swivel his head, keep an eye on his surroundings, was hard to ignore. But Tate trusted the Desparre officers he'd worked with for the past five and a half years. This wasn't Boston. Besides, both he and Sabrina wore bulletproof vests beneath their lightweight jackets.

He was a little overheated walking in the sunshine. Or maybe it was just from his proximity to Sabrina.

Except for the weight of that vest and the knowledge that his colleagues were hiding nearby and watching his every move, everything about this felt right. A natural progression of the attraction he'd felt from the moment he'd met Sabrina.

Getting to know her more over the past week had only intensified those feelings.

He glanced at her, taking in things he'd noticed the first time he'd seen her: the way the sun cast a golden sheen over her wavy hair, the natural elegance of her face, the depths of her green eyes. But also seeing new things now that she'd truly let him in: the way her lips tightened at the corners when she was stressed. The flush that rose easily to her cheeks when she was flustered or embarrassed. The way her gaze was always moving, taking everything in and strategizing. For someone who made a living in creative arts, she was analytical enough to run through police strategy with him. And successfully evade a stalker for two years on her own.

A swell of pride filled him, even though he had no right to it. Without conscious intent, he squeezed her hand, and she looked his way.

Her smile was equal parts shy uncertainty and knowing amusement. But it was probably hard to miss the effect she had on him. Even his chief had picked up on it, used it as the basis to suggest this pretense.

"Sabrina!" From one of the intact benches near the park, Lora had spotted them. She came running and Tate took a deep breath.

They were about to discover if their ruse was working.

He hadn't been thrilled about telling Lora

their suspicions about Adam, but after his call to her, it had seemed like the best approach. She'd promised to keep it to herself and although she was often in everyone's business, she was trustworthy. Still, he and the chief had agreed it was best not to give her any more detail than they had to, including the truth about his and Sabrina's supposed relationship.

Lora slowed slightly as she approached, her gaze dropping speculatively to Sabrina's and Tate's linked hands before she threw her arms around Sabrina's neck.

Sabrina was knocked back a step by the force of it, and Tate dropped her hand. While she was distracted, he glanced around.

Nothing seemed out of the ordinary. Just another day in downtown Desparre. There were more people out than usual because of the brilliant sunshine, but not so many that Adam would be able to hide in a crowd.

Then again, he knew his fellow officers were close, and he didn't see them. The sliver of anxiety he'd felt since they stepped outside grew, and he wished for Sitka's comforting presence. His K-9 partner was back at his house, since Tate was pretending to be off work. He'd initially argued to bring her, but the chief had overruled him, saying he didn't want to provide a reason for a group of kids to surround Sitka and distract them.

"I'm so sorry," Lora exclaimed, squeezing Sabrina's hand and looking upset. "I had no idea… I believed Adam when he said he'd grown up in Alaska. He knew so much about the state. And his wife—"

"Don't worry," Sabrina interrupted, her smile almost reaching her eyes. "We're not completely sure it was him, but whoever it was, the police seem to have scared him off. And the upside of it all…"

She took Tate's hand again, and he stepped closer, returning the soft smile she gave him.

"I met Tate," she concluded, an upward lilt to her voice that made the whole thing sound even more real.

He wished it was.

He'd shared things with Sabrina he hadn't shared with anyone in a long time. Pieces of his life that he'd been purposely evasive about with colleagues, even those people he called his friends. But after a week of dinners in her hotel room, there'd been only so long they could discuss the investigation, only so many awkward attempts at chitchat before she'd dived in with real questions. He'd looked into parts of her life without her consent, so he figured he owed her some truths, too, even if he couldn't give her all the details.

She was the only person here who knew how badly he missed talking to his parents, their respective partners, and even his mom's boyfriend's kids, who were younger than him and he hadn't grown up with but were all nice. She didn't understand his vague excuses for not having seen them in over five years, but the rest of it had been true. She understood because she missed her family, too.

Their connection went deeper than their shared experience—especially since she didn't even know they shared one. As he watched her smile and tell Lora the story about how they'd started dating, he wished he'd asked Sabrina out the first time he'd met her. Their relationship still would have had an expiration date, but at least it would have been real.

The ache that filled him at that moment must have shown on his face, because Lora shifted her attention to him. As he attempted a smile to cover up whatever she'd seen, she let out a surprised laugh.

"You know, the first time Sabrina admitted she thought you were cute, I told her to go for it. But I thought you were too much of a loner to ever get involved."

Her assessment of him stung a bit, but it was hard to focus on that part. He grinned at Sabrina, couldn't help himself from nudging her the way he might if he was actually dating her. "You thought I was cute, huh?"

She flushed an even deeper red, but instead of mumbling something vague like he'd expected, she countered, "Yep. But it was Sitka who pushed you over the edge and got you a date."

A surprised laugh escaped. "Figures. Everyone always tells me she's the better-looking one in the partnership."

Lora laughed at that, then gave Sabrina another hug. "I should let you two enjoy your date." She glanced from Sabrina to him and back again. "I'm happy for you, Sabrina. You deserve this." Then she leaned in and hugged Tate. "I think you do, too, Tate."

As she walked away, Tate glanced at Sabrina again. She was smiling at him, amusement and something that looked like longing on her face.

The longer he stared into her eyes, the more the amusement dropped away until she swayed slightly forward.

He felt himself lean toward her instinctively and then forced himself to straighten, squeeze her hand and tug her forward again. He made his voice overly cheerful, overly loud. "Want to walk around the park?"

It was a reminder to himself as much as her that most of the Desparre police department was watching them right now. As much as he wanted to kiss her, he didn't want to do it in front of an audience. And he didn't want to do it when it wasn't real.

At least if Adam was watching, he should have no doubt that they were a couple.

Sabrina blinked a few times, the desire there fading away until she gave him a tentative smile. "Sure."

As they continued down the street, regret welled up. Regret that he hadn't given in to the moment and kissed her. Regret that he couldn't tell her the full truth about who he was. But even more than that, regret that their time was limited.

Because once they arrested her stalker, she'd be leaving. And he couldn't follow. New York was too close to Boston to ever be safe for him.

AFTER TWO FULL days of flaunting her supposed relationship with Tate all over town, Sabrina was exhausted. And Adam—if he was still here—hadn't taken the bait.

Still, as she walked beside Tate around the cute set of shops outside downtown, hyperaware of the feel of his hand in hers, she didn't care if Adam took a week to make his move. The outdoor shopping center, a quirky assortment of stores that seemed to have holiday lights on the roofs year-round, was normally one of her favorite spots. But she couldn't focus on them with Tate beside her.

If she squinted a little, she could make their surroundings go blurry and just keep Tate in focus. If only there were a way to do that with her life. Make all the challenges drop away and just be here with him for real.

For the first time in two years, it felt like someone actually *knew* her again. Sharing more and more about herself with him each night seemed right. Even if she'd met him back in New York, surrounded by plenty of friends and family, she would have wanted him in her life.

"What made you decide to become a cop?" The words popped out of her mouth without her even realizing she'd been thinking them. But it was something she'd wondered about since the moment that truck had raced toward Sitka, and again later, when she'd heard Tate had been knocked off his feet chasing Mario McKeever.

He seemed surprised by the question, but then his steps slowed slightly, something she'd come to recognize he did when he got serious.

"I told you my parents divorced when I was young." When she nodded, he continued. "I wouldn't say it was an ugly divorce, not compared to the things I've seen as a cop. But as a seven-year-old, it felt scary. It seemed like all they did was argue, and I was always in the middle. They shared custody, which in the long run, I'm glad about. But at the time, it felt like as soon as I got settled in one house, I was shuttled to the other."

"I'm sorry," Sabrina said when he paused, his lips pursed, his forehead creasing. "My dad took off when I was five. Totally different thing, because he spent most of my childhood chasing after the next new thing—usually his next girlfriend or his next car. He reappears every few years, wanting to reestablish a relationship. Even as an adult, it's disorienting. And honestly, I saw him occasionally, but I'm not that interested. It's not much of a bond when it's all on one person's terms."

He squeezed her hand. "I'm glad you had your mom and brother. And I'm glad you'll get back to them soon."

His words sent a pang through her—a desperate longing to see her family mixed with dread at the thought of leaving him behind.

Maybe he saw how conflicted she suddenly felt, because he cleared his throat and started walking again. She hadn't even realized they'd stopped.

"So, dealing with my parents' divorce made me angry, frustrated." His lips tilted downward as he added, "Lonely. And just adrift. My dad had already moved across town, into a different school district. Then mom couldn't afford our old house by herself. She moved closer to my dad, thinking it would be easier. But it meant I also had to change schools, and I started getting bullied."

Sabrina put her free hand against his arm. "That's a lot to deal with all at once. I'm sorry you went through that."

He gave her a quick smile that seemed to say *Don't worry*. It was so typically Tate that she couldn't help but smile back. The smile faded as he looked forward again, kept talking. How had she gotten to know what all of his smiles meant? How had it happened so quickly?

She'd known him for just over two weeks. They weren't even *actually* dating, and already, she felt more connected to him than she had with Dylan after three months.

The thought made guilt rush through her. She tried to push it back, to just focus on this moment, on this man. Even if it wasn't real, it was the best thing she'd had in her life in years.

"I started getting into fights, too." At the surprised glance she shot him, he laughed. "I know. It's out of character. It was then, too. My parents didn't know what to do with me. Then one day I was walking home from school, and a group of kids started beating up on me."

Sabrina gasped, and he squeezed her hand again.

"I was ten then, I think. Three years of struggling at school and at home and letting my anger get the best of me. A police officer stopped his car, sirens flashing. All those kids took off *fast*. I wasn't in any shape to go anywhere, so the cop gave me a ride home. He talked to me about channeling anger the right way, about making the right choices even when the people around me are making the wrong ones. It made an impression."

Sabrina tried to imagine a younger Tate, angry and hurting. She pictured him at ten, his light brown skin covered in bruises, his deep brown eyes—always so intuitive and kind—filled with cynicism and frustration. "Did you stay in touch with him?"

"It wasn't *that* big a town. Even if I hadn't wanted to, he would have found me." Tate laughed. "He retired a couple of years ago down to Florida." The fondness in his tone faded to something wishful. "I haven't talked to him in a while."

"Maybe you should call him," Sabrina suggested, wishing the solutions were so simple for the people she missed.

He paused, regret flitting across his face before he smiled down at her. "Yeah, I should."

She stared back at him, wondering if there was any way to turn what they had into something real. If he could stay connected with his friend in Florida, he could do the same for her in New York. Maybe he'd want to visit, let her show him around. Could they build a relationship from that long a distance?

Then again, did it make any sense to let someone like Tate go over something as simple as geography?

Her pulse picked up as he continued to stare at her, as if he was trying to read her mind. But wondering if he'd ever leave Alaska if they got serious was getting ridiculously ahead of herself. They'd never broached the idea of dating for real. They'd never even *kissed*.

His gaze darted to her lips.

Could he read her mind? A smile trembled on her lips, and each breath came faster as it occurred to her. What better way to see how Tate felt about her? And as an added bonus, maybe it would finally give Adam the incentive he needed to take the bait.

Before she lost her courage, Sabrina fisted her free hand in Tate's T-shirt, pulling him downward and swiveling him toward her all at once. She grinned at the surprise that flashed in his eyes, followed immediately by a dark intensity that told her he wanted to kiss her, too.

Dropping his T-shirt, she pulled her other hand free from his and slid both of her hands slowly up his arms, holding his gaze. His eyelids dropped and his muscles flexed under her fingers, emboldening her. She kept going, leaning up on her tiptoes as she slipped her hands beneath the sleeves of his shirt. She vaguely registered the feel of puckered, uneven skin beneath her left hand, and then his lips were pressed against hers.

They were soft, even fuller than she'd realized. Electricity buzzed over her skin as he brushed his lips against hers, once, twice, before sliding his tongue across the seam of her mouth.

She sank against him, gripping his shoulders as his hands clamped onto her hips and raised her up more. Opening her mouth, she invited him in, flicking her tongue against his as her body flushed at the feel of him against her.

Then, too quickly, he was setting her away from him, his hands on her biceps, the apology in his eyes not hiding the desire. "Maybe we should do this without an audience," he suggested, his voice huskier than usual.

A smile broke free, echoing the hope bursting in her chest. He shared her feelings. She could see it in his gaze, feel it in his touch.

Maybe she wasn't a fool to think about a future with him. Maybe, thanks to him, she could finally *have* a future.

Before she could voice any of the things she was thinking, he frowned and dug into his pocket. Then, he was holding his phone out for her to read a text message from Chief Griffith.

I don't know if Adam left or if he's just not taking the bait with so many people around.

Sabrina glanced around the sparsely populated shops. She could see Officer Nate Dreymond in plainclothes pretending to window-shop down the street, a couple arguing about their weekend coming out of the shop next to them, and a handful of people wandering in and out of stores. It was less busy than the park where Adam had set Talise's truck on Sitka. Then again, maybe he was worried the police were watching. Maybe he suspected it was a trap. She glanced down at the rest of the text.

We have a new plan. Something that will look like an easier mark for Adam. You and Sabrina pretend to go away on a romantic weekend together.

Chapter Seventeen

"His real name is Adam Locklay," Tate announced as Sabrina opened the door to her hotel room.

He paused to hand her the tea and muffin he'd picked up for her in the hotel's restaurant, taking in her hair, which seemed more wavy and untamed than usual. From the sleepy way she blinked at him, she hadn't been awake long. He paused to take in a fresh-from-sleep Sabrina as she seemed to register what he'd said.

"What?" Her voice was barely above a whisper as Sitka pushed past him and sat at Sabrina's feet, wagging her tail.

Sabrina's eyes were wide enough to momentarily distract him with their various shades of green, shifting from emerald to moss. The scent of the tea he'd bought her wafted toward him, along with the faint smell of vanilla. Her shampoo or lotion? Whatever it was, it was as distracting as the rest of her.

Closing the door behind him, he asked, "Does the name mean something to you?"

"No. How did you figure it out?"

"By spending a lot of time on social media. Using that picture I found, we identified other people in the background close to Adam and dug into their social media until we finally got to a picture where he was tagged. With his real name, we could dig up a lot more about him, too."

As Sitka gave a short whine, Sabrina smiled briefly at his dog, absently petting her. "I can't believe I finally have a real name to put to these years of notes and…" She lifted her hand, palm up, as if she couldn't sum up all of the horror of her past two and a half years.

He slid his hand underneath her upturned palm and she flipped it over to entwine their hands. "A name is the first step. We're on *his* tail now. It's a matter of time before we catch up to him."

"I hope so." She glanced down at their linked hands, then up at him, and he could see the questions in her eyes.

Questions about that kiss they'd shared yesterday. About his suggestion that they hit pause until they were alone again.

They were alone *now*.

Nerves tightened his chest, and anticipation quickened his breathing. She'd always seemed shy, so despite the heated looks she'd been giving him, he'd been shocked when she'd grabbed him and kissed him yesterday. And damn, she really could kiss.

His gaze dropped to her lips, and her tongue darted out to wet them, making him sway forward. But he caught himself before he pulled her to him.

He hadn't come here to finish something he

never should have let her start. He'd come to talk about the status of their search for Adam and their plan to finally lure him out of hiding and end the threat against Sabrina for good.

Letting go of her hand, he stepped around her and set his take-out coffee on the table, giving himself a chance to refocus. He leaned against the wall, putting a little space between them. "Adam Locklay moved out to New York for college and stuck around. He's got a history of stalking."

Sabrina set her tea and muffin on the table beside her bed, moving toward him.

Sitka stuck close to Sabrina's side, her tail wagging. His dog stared up at Sabrina happily, the way she did with him at home, when she was relaxed and off duty. She was going to miss Sabrina as much as he was.

"He's done this to other women?"

She sounded furious on their behalf, and it made him like her even more. She'd spent two and a half years afraid for herself, afraid for the people she loved because of Adam, and here she was, mad that he'd dared to make anyone else feel that way.

"Yeah." He tried not to get distracted by her approach, by thoughts of how little time he might have left to spend with her. "But as far as we can tell, never like this. In the past, he stalked women he knew. Two ex-girlfriends and one coworker, who all went to the police. Two of them ended up with restraining orders against him, and one called the police multiple times because of incidents, usually him stopping by unwanted and refusing to leave."

"Any violence?" Sabrina asked, her tone hesitant, like she was afraid to hear who else he'd killed chasing the objects of his obsession.

"None that I could find. He escalated with you."

"Aren't I lucky," she muttered darkly.

The only one who was lucky in any of this was him. If Adam hadn't stalked her, then Tate never would have met her. She would have gone on with her life in New York, gone on dating Dylan Westwood, maybe even married him.

Even the idea of never having the chance to know her put an uncomfortable tightness in Tate's chest that made it hard to take a full breath. But he wished Adam had never set eyes on her, wished Sabrina had never known this terror.

When he didn't immediately answer, she stepped a little closer, sending another waft of vanilla his way, and asked, "Have you been able to track his movements? Has he been behind me this whole time?"

"I don't think so. We don't know how he found you, but there's evidence he was still in New York five months ago. He works as an independent software developer, and he's able to work from home, so it's possible he's been traveling and returning to New York. But given what you've told me about all the places you've been, I have to think he found you here and then followed."

Her shoulders jerked, and she let out a huff. "Of all the places I've hidden, this one is the most remote. The place I felt most safe. The place that felt most like *home*."

Something pensive crossed her face, some emotion he tried to latch onto but couldn't quite read.

It wasn't fair to her not to keep his distance. But he couldn't seem to stop himself from moving a little closer. "This *is* your home, at least right now. It's your town. And we look out for each other here. We're going to find him. It just…" He frowned, trying to figure out the best way to tell her, then decided straightforward was the best approach. She'd managed the threat alone for two years. She could handle his other news.

"It just might take a little longer than we'd hoped. Which is why I think the plan the chief mentioned yesterday is a good one. If you're okay with it, we're getting things prepped right now. In two days, it will be set up."

Sabrina stared at him a minute, like she wasn't sure which part of that to question first. Finally, she asked, "Why will it take longer?"

"We assumed Adam's stories about living in Alaska were all lies." When shock and compassion crossed Sabrina's face, Tate rushed on. "And they were. He was never married. You don't need to feel sorry for his loss. We suspect he made it up as a way to connect with you, to get you to talk about your own loss."

Grief and fury flashed across Sabrina's face in rapid succession, and Tate felt an answering pang of sympathy. Adam had killed someone she cared about and then tried to connect with her by pretending a similar loss.

Sabrina clamped a hand against her stomach. "He was hoping I'd talk to him about Dylan's death, never knowing he'd actually caused it? That's even sicker than the notes."

"I know. I'm sorry."

Lines creased Sabrina's forehead as she wrapped her arms around her middle, seeming to sink inward. "I'm glad I never did."

But he could hear it in her words. She'd thought about it, thought Adam was someone who'd understand her loss.

Cursing inwardly, Tate readied himself to give her more bad news. "He never lived here, either. The thing is, he was probably able to convince someone like Lora who *did* grow up here, and in the mountains, no less, because the wilderness isn't foreign to him. He grew up in Michigan's upper peninsula, with parents who were known to have some survivalist mentality."

"He understood how to hide here," Sabrina summarized. "That explains why he was so comfortable trekking through the woods to spy on me."

"Yes," Tate confirmed. He took another step closer, until all he'd need to do was reach out and take her hands in his, pull her to him and hold her until the worry and betrayal left her face. He wanted to, especially when his movement made heat spark in her gaze again.

He wanted to forget all of his good intentions of remaining professional, helping her reclaim her life without making it even harder to say goodbye. He wanted to feel her lips on his again, wanted to run his hands through her hair and walk her to the bed that was way too close. Instead, he fisted his hands at his side.

From the way Sitka's gaze moved from him to Sabrina, he couldn't even fool his dog.

The last of the anger left her face as her lips twitched with sudden amusement. "So you want to go away with me for the weekend, then." Her tone was teasing, but her gaze was serious as she moved close, slid her hands up his arms. The soft glide of her fingertips and the mix of nerves and desire in her eyes weakened his resolve.

Her fingers stalled on the edges of the scar hidden by the sleeve of his T-shirt. "What happened here?"

"A danger of the job," he answered, a semi-truth because he didn't want to outright lie to her.

"Gunshot wound." At her gasp, he added, "It was a long time ago. And it just skimmed me."

Summoning his willpower, he took a step back, watching the confusion in her eyes as he said, "I don't want you to worry. You're not going to be in danger. We have two days to set this up right. This is going to be a trap for Adam."

She bit the edge of her lip, then whispered, "I'm not worried. I feel safe with you."

Her words sent a rush through him even before she moved forward again. This time, she was less hesitant, giving him a shaky smile before she pressed her hands against his chest.

His arms twitched at the contact, and her smile grew more confident as she leaned into him, replacing her hands with the length of her body. "I think it will work."

It took him a minute to take his focus off the feel of her pressed against him and understand her words. "I think so, too." Adam was less likely to be able to resist if he and Sabrina were supposedly alone.

"And once he's no longer a threat—" she slid her arms around his waist and leaned back slightly to stare up at him "—I was hoping you and I could try this for real."

His mouth went dry, and for an instant, he couldn't breathe. The desire to nod and press his lips against hers was overwhelming, but how could he make a promise he couldn't keep? Even though there was no indication Kevin or Paul had found him as a result of the news article, he'd planned to leave town as soon as he'd eliminated the threat of her stalker. Even if he decided it was safe enough to stay in Alaska, what would he say when she inevitably wanted him to come see her in New York? What if he got too close to Boston again and the threats against him became a danger to her?

"I can't," he said, his voice a scratchy whisper.

She flushed deep red and backed out of his arms as Sitka whimpered and nudged up against her, eyeing Tate like he'd just become the enemy.

"I'm sorry. I want to. You have no idea..." He took a deep breath, trying to be as honest as he could. "But Desparre is a long way from New York City."

She nodded, ducking her head as she backed farther away.

An ache settled in his gut, for hurting her, for saying no when he so desperately wanted to say yes. But it wasn't right. He'd come to care about her too much to hurt her. In the long run, pursuing a relationship with Sabrina could make her the target of someone new. The threat against him might never end.

"I promised to give you your life back." He stepped closer, tipping her chin up with his hand even as he longed to pull her back into his arms.

"I won't stop until I do it. But that means leaving everything in Alaska behind. Including me."

NERVES CHURNED IN Sabrina's stomach as she waited for Tate to come to her hotel room and pick her up for their supposed romantic weekend away together.

Three days ago, when she'd kissed him in the street, their pretending had felt so natural, so *real*. When he'd said he wanted to continue what she'd started in private, she thought he felt all the same things she did. So when he'd shown up the next morning and insisted long-distance would never work, it had been a shock. Embarrassing. And devastating.

Yet, he'd kept coming to see her the next two evenings, bringing dinner and smiling at her like nothing had happened. She'd tried to smile back, act as unaffected as he appeared, but *that* pretending had left her exhausted and depressed.

At least he'd continued to bring Sitka with him. The sweet dog definitely sensed something was wrong, and she'd spent a lot of the visits at Sabrina's feet, her head perched on Sabrina's knees. She would miss Sitka when she left, too.

Despite everything, she still believed their plan could work. Adam had gone after Dylan the day she was meeting his family for the first time. Back then, she'd thought it was a terrible coincidence. But now, knowing how closely he could have been watching her in her cabin? Remembering how he'd managed to slip a note into her purse even after the police had been on high alert trying to find him back in New York? He'd probably known.

She'd been about to take a serious step in a relationship, and he'd stopped it. Given how much she and Tate had been spreading news about their intended getaway to a secluded cabin, she had to believe he'd repeat that pattern.

Her nerves intensified, shifted into fear that made her breathing way too fast. "Relax," she told herself. Tate was a trained police officer. And they wouldn't be alone. Much of the Desparre PD would be hidden nearby, ready to take Adam down.

It would work. It had to work. Because Tate was right. It was time for her to go home.

Acute homesickness swept through her, pricking her eyes with tears. Without conscious thought, she moved toward her phone. She'd never dared to go onto social media, hadn't wanted to sign into an account that might leave some kind of trail. But if Tate had been able to see details about her brother...

Pulling up Conor's social-media account without signing in, she realized he'd made a lot of his posts public. Her stockbroker brother, who lived by numbers and rules and always warned her about keeping her personal information locked up, had purposely left pieces of his life open to the world.

As she scrolled through, so fast the pictures and posts were nothing more than quick glimpses, she realized he'd done it two years ago. A way for her to stay connected with them, no matter how far she ran. And she'd never known, never even thought to check, because she'd been focused on pure survival.

Conor's face blurred, and she swiped at the tears that had welled in her eyes as she scrolled back to the top of his feed. His latest post, dated yesterday, showed him beaming beside Jie, his longtime girlfriend. Jie was grinning, one hand held up to the camera, showing off a sparkling diamond.

They'd gotten engaged. Finally. They'd met in college, dated ever since. In the year or two before Sabrina had run, she could tell Jie was starting to get frustrated. They'd been together a long time. She wanted to get married and have kids. Conor was dragging his feet.

Sabrina got it. Their dad had taken off when she was five and Conor was seven. While she and Conor had watched their mom struggle to make ends meet, to try to fill the void their father had left, their dad had jumped from one woman to the next, carefree. He'd appeared every few months, or sometimes every few years, and dropped off presents, wanted to take them out. It hadn't really put Sabrina off the idea of marriage, but from a young age, Conor had vowed never to wed.

Jie was so good for her brother. Sabrina had been worried he would lose her if he didn't make that commitment. Now the leap of faith had happened. And she'd missed it. Still, a bittersweet smile pulled her lips at the happiness radiating from that picture.

Maybe she'd make it back to New York for the wedding. The idea buoyed her, took away some of the pain of seeing all she'd missed. She scrolled more, seeing birthdays and holidays. More happiness, but she could see it on everyone's faces that they missed her as much as she missed them.

Then she found a picture of Conor and her mom from a few weeks earlier, smiling in Central Park, and a sharp pain clamped back down on her chest. She ran her finger over the side of her mom's face, seeing new lines at the corners of her mouth and across her forehead. She looked like she'd experienced way too much sadness in the past two years. Conor, too, looked older, more weary.

Sabrina had done this to them by leaving. If she had to go back and make the same decision now, she'd do it again. But she was tired of being forced to choose safety over happiness.

There was a familiar knock at the door, a particular beat she recognized as Tate's, followed by Sitka's enthusiastic *woof!*

Closing the browser on her phone, she stood and took a deep breath.

It was long past time she made a stand for herself and reclaimed the life she'd left behind.

Chapter Eighteen

"Hi," Sabrina breathed, feeling a flush creep up her neck and cheeks at the shy, uncertain tone of her voice. Clearing her throat, she opened the hotel door wider.

Sitka rushed inside at the invitation, running around Sabrina in a circle that made her laugh.

Tate smiled, something hesitant in his gaze, but he couldn't seem to help a laugh at his dog's antics. "She's a pro at work, but get her off duty and she's a big goofball."

Woof! Sitka glanced back at him briefly, then returned her attention to Sabrina.

"You know you are," Tate teased his dog as Sabrina leaned down to pet Sitka and hide her face behind a curtain of hair.

This was the Tate she wanted to know better. The Tate who teased his dog, who made her feel safe and excited at the same time. Even knowing that today was all for show, it was too easy to imagine a version of this that was real. The idea of going on an actual romantic weekend away with him made her pulse pick up again.

Her attraction wasn't one-sided, that much she knew for sure. But Tate was too practical and realistic, probably the result of being a police officer—or maybe why he'd become one. She, on the other hand, had always indulged her creative, fanciful impulses. It was how she'd ended up in fashion design and now, finally, jewelry-making. More than once, those impulses had led her to take a chance on the wrong relationship. But until Adam had forced his way into her life, she'd lived without fear.

She hadn't been irresponsible. Her mom had drilled into her from a young age the need to be diligent about safety. But she'd refused to let her dad's leaving color the way she looked at relationships just like she'd refused to let her mom's overprotectiveness and caution send her into a safe, staid career instead of the uncertain field of creative arts that she loved.

After six months of notes and then Dylan's murder, she'd lost too much of that freedom to fear. Tate made her want to toss aside caution, toss aside her own pride and go after what she wanted, no matter the obstacles.

Sitka gave a sudden wet slosh of her tongue over Sabrina's cheek, as if she knew what Sabrina was thinking and was on board. Laughing, Sabrina wiped away the dampness, pet Sitka once more, then stood.

It was still awkward, with Tate standing there, looking way too tempting in black pants and a T-shirt that didn't hide the lean muscles underneath. At least some of her embarrassment had faded, and her face no longer felt like it was on fire.

She'd kissed him. He'd ultimately rejected her. But that didn't mean she had to give up.

The idea brought a slow smile to her face, and he swayed backward slightly, as if he'd felt the sudden force of her determination. Still, he gave her a smile in return, then asked loudly, "You ready to go?"

Then she realized something. Usually, he closed and locked the door as soon as he arrived. Today, it was wide open. She didn't see anyone in the hallway behind him, but that didn't mean Adam wasn't somewhere nearby.

Shoving back a surge of fear, she nodded and grabbed her duffel bag, packed with enough clothes and toiletries for the weekend. Hopefully, Adam would take the bait early and not make her and Tate play out a whole weekend of this awkward farce with all of Tate's colleagues watching. If he didn't, maybe she should take advantage of it, see if she could change Tate's mind.

The idea gained traction as he reached over and took her bag, slinging it easily over his shoulder. Then he took her hand in his and pulled her toward the door.

She sidled closer to him, the way she'd do if they were really dating, and he shot her a quick glance, full of surprise and heat, before calling, "Come on, Sitka."

The dog raced after them, sticking close to Sabrina as they took the elevator down to the lobby.

Even where no one could see them, Tate kept his hold on her hand. But his gaze was focused on the closed door.

She could see his reflection in the shiny metal, the stern set of his jaw, the stiffness of his posture, the seriousness in his gaze. But his fingers slid back and forth over her knuckles, a soothing caress she wasn't sure he was aware he was giving.

As the numbers on the elevator readout counted down, Sabrina tilted her head and rested it against Tate's arm. She breathed in his familiar sandalwood scent and closed her eyes, trying to mentally prepare for the weekend ahead.

The idea of spending any romantic time with Tate—even if it was pretend—made her pulse quicken. But it couldn't eliminate the building fear.

Adam was still out there, still obsessed with her and presumably still willing to kill anyone who got in his way.

Her hand clenched reflexively in Tate's as the elevator dinged and came to a stop.

"You okay?" Tate whispered as the doors slid open.

"Yes." She opened her eyes and took a deep breath, leading him through the lobby. "Let's do this."

"Hang on a second," he said, tugging on her hand just as they stepped outside. With a sudden grin, he pulled a cap from his back pocket, showed her the logo for a police K-9 training facility. "I got us a nice, secluded cabin where you'll be able to see the mountains and water, and even a glacier. But this is still Alaska, not New York City." He settled the cap on her head, then nodded. "Now you fit in."

She gave him a perplexed smile, glancing down at her simple jeans and top. Okay, yes, her jeans were slim and showed off her figure, and her top was a piece she'd found at one of the quirky shops in Desparre, flowy and lacy and the same green as her eyes. She'd swiped on some lipstick and a couple of coats of mascara before he arrived. But she wasn't exactly decked out for a party in the city.

Instead of asking about it, she turned toward his truck, parked out front. She itched to glance around, reassure herself that other police officers were keeping watch, but she resisted. If Adam was nearby, she didn't want to tip him off.

Before she could get more than a step, Tate was tugging on her hand again, pulling her back to him. "I'm glad we're doing this," he told her, his voice dropping to a husky whisper.

His eyes locked on hers as he threaded his free hand through her hair, then cupped the base of her neck. The feel of his fingers made her nerve endings spark to life, sending zings of electricity through her body.

He dipped his head slowly, the intensity in his eyes telling her he wanted to kiss her, even if the location said this was all for show. To prove to Adam it was real, to goad him into making his move.

Looping her free hand around his neck, she rose up on her tiptoes to meet him. Surprise flashed briefly in his eyes, followed by desire, and then his lips settled softly against hers.

He tasted faintly of coffee underneath mint toothpaste. The scent of sandalwood she'd started to crave when he wasn't around filled her senses as she closed her eyes and gave in to his kiss. Gave in to the intoxicating feel of his body pressed against hers, the way she could rest all of her weight on him and he'd hold steady. Gave in to all of the emotions she'd been trying to deny.

He paused for half a second, and then his hand slipped free of hers to clamp onto her hip, to haul her higher onto her tiptoes against him. His fingers flexed there, kneading into her hip as he nipped at her lips with his mouth and tongue. Then his tongue slid between her lips, sending sparks down to her toes.

She hung on tighter, linking her hands at the back of his neck as she urged him with the slide of her tongue to go faster. She felt frantic, desperate to get closer to him, as all of the dreams she'd started to envision of a future with him swept over her. Maybe those dreams were possible. Or maybe this was her one chance to create a memory with him.

Either way, she wasn't going to waste it. She tried to slow down, to memorize the imprint of his body against hers, the slight rasp of his chin as his mouth claimed hers over and over.

Too soon, he eased back, and she dropped down to her feet, tugging on her shirt where it had ridden up slightly. He stared at her, a mix of surprise and uncertainty in his gaze, until Sitka made them both jump with a sudden *woof!*

"You're right," Tate said, shifting his gaze to the dog and breaking the spell. "We should get going. You don't mind Sitka joining us for our romantic weekend, do you?"

He looked at her again, and even though his gaze was more controlled, his emotions veiled again, he let out a heavy breath that told her he wasn't as composed as he was pretending.

She gave him a knowing smile. "Of course not." Threading her hand through his, she said, loudly enough to be overheard, "I'm ready."

He blinked at her again, his forehead creasing as if he wasn't sure if he should be reading into her words or not.

Letting him wonder, she tugged on his hand as Sitka trotted along beside her toward the truck.

He held open the door for her, then warned, "It's a little tight in the cab for three. I'm sorry about that. I've never needed to fit an extra person in here with us."

He'd only had Sitka a few months. But the way he said it made it sound like he'd never taken another woman on a romantic getaway like this—at least not while he'd had this truck. Maybe she was reading into it, but the idea made her smile.

The dog leaped into the truck, settling into the middle and taking up some of Sabrina's seat, too.

Sabrina stepped up after her, settling her hand on Sitka's back as Tate closed her door and went around to the driver's side.

On top of everything else, he was a gentleman. Of course, maybe that was part of the problem. Part of the reason he was so determined to do what was right and practical by not jumping into anything when they were trying to make it safe for her to leave.

How could she change his mind? The distance from Desparre to New York City was no joke. And this town could easily snow you in through winter. But she didn't care. She wanted to try.

Maybe Adam would wait, give her at least part of the weekend to show Tate that the bond they'd developed was worth the effort, worth the challenges. But when the truck came to a stop ten minutes later, she realized she wasn't sure how.

Glancing around with surprise, she took in the cute house with the big front porch in the woods. It was much closer than she'd expected. Then the garage door in front of them opened, and Sabrina realized they weren't at the vacation spot he'd mentioned at all but his house.

She turned toward him, questions forming, as he turned off the truck and shut the garage door behind him.

Then the door leading to his house opened, and a woman stepped into the garage. She had wavy blond hair and wore a cap identical to the one Tate had slid onto Sabrina's head. She was even wearing the same jeans and green blouse—the outfit she'd shown Tate two days ago when he'd asked what she planned to wear. Until this moment, she'd never really wondered why he'd asked.

Realization about what was happening hit at the same time as the knowledge that she wouldn't get a chance to convince Tate of anything. Because she wasn't going on the romantic getaway with him at all.

TATE WAS DOING the right thing. He knew he was.

Still, as he glanced across the truck at the rookie police officer from nearby Luna—on loan because she looked enough like Sabrina to pass for her—dread clamped down and refused to leave. He gave her a forced smile, trying to reassure her. "There are officers already in place around the cabin. We'll be fine."

"I'm not worried," she said, an echo of the

words Sabrina had told him earlier, her face strategically hidden behind an open map.

Unlike Sabrina, Officer Angie Hallen didn't quite sound like she meant them.

He'd been a rookie once, on foot patrol back in Boston, with a veteran officer whose training method was to toss you into the fray and hope you came out in one piece. He remembered the adrenaline and the nerves all too well. Time and experience calmed both, but if you were smart, they never fully dulled, because losing your edge on the job could cost your life.

"I appreciate you agreeing to do this," he told her. Angie didn't know the Desparre officers, and although she'd been briefed on the threat, she didn't have a history with him, didn't know what kind of officer he was.

Then again, he knew all too well that sometimes even people you knew and trusted could become a threat.

Angie nodded stiffly, and Sitka, maybe noticing her nerves, or maybe just missing Sabrina, let out a whine.

"We'll be there soon," he told his dog.

The romantic getaway spot was well-known among Desparre locals and would be easy for Adam to figure out. It was on the far southern border of Desparre, an hour away from downtown. People who weren't used to the area tended to be shocked when they suddenly came out of the woods and upon another, smaller mountain, this one edged with water and a small glacier.

Sabrina would have loved it. The thought popped into his mind and wouldn't leave, along with an image of the look in her eyes when she'd fallen into his arms and taken his kiss to a whole other level. But the look on her face when she realized she wasn't coming with him? That one stung. He'd seen a hint of betrayal, along with regret. The same regret he was feeling now.

Her kisses had held more than simple passion. There had been a promise in them, a glimpse of what he could have if he gave in to what they both wanted.

There was an ache in his chest just thinking about what he was giving up. But he needed to find a way to just be happy they were going to get her life back. Because as he glanced once more at Angie, tensing as their cabin came into view, he felt it in his gut. Adam was going to take the bait.

Even though it meant saying goodbye to Sabrina, Tate couldn't help feeling a sharp anticipation at the idea of snapping a pair of handcuffs on Adam and throwing him behind bars for good.

He pulled into the drive of the cabin he'd rented, far from the others scattered along the glacier's edge. Officers Riera and Dreymond had already picked up the key for him, letting the owners know to stay away. So now all he had to do was grab his and Sabrina's bags from the back of his truck. Then he tucked Angie into the crook of his arm, her face hidden against his chest, and hustled her into the cabin. With one sharp whistle, Sitka raced in after them.

Shutting and locking the door behind him, Tate did a quick check of the cabin, confirming it was empty and secure and that all the shades were drawn. "We're good," he told Angie as he returned to the main room.

She nodded and tucked her pistol back into the waistband at the back of her jeans. "Good. Let's check in with your backup."

"Our backup," he reminded her, grabbing his cell phone from his bag. He sent a quick text to Lorenzo Riera, and the response came back almost immediately.

We've got you. Stay alert.

"They're in place," Tate told Angie. "Now let's hope Adam makes his move quickly."

He settled onto the couch across from the front door, which gave him good visibility into the bedroom and the window access there. Then, he raised his eyebrow at Angie as she stood by the door, knowing that even though he wanted a fast resolution, this kind of operation was often a waiting game.

"I'm good here," she told him.

An hour later, she pulled a chair next to the

couch and sat stiffly in it. An hour after that, she started pacing. Ten hours after that, she was slouched on the other side of the couch. By then, Tate was ready to do the same. But he also knew the darkness was Adam's friend, a time when he might feel safer sneaking up on the woman he'd been stalking and her new police-officer boyfriend.

So, when his cell phone rang, he grabbed it fast. "Talk to me," he told Lorenzo, hoping the veteran officer had already wrestled Adam to the ground and slapped cuffs on him.

"It's... We're—" The sound of gunshots made Angie jerk beside him just as Tate realized it wasn't Lorenzo, hiding in the woods with most of the Desparre officers.

It was Charlie Quinn, who was back at Tate's house, keeping Sabrina safe.

He leaped to his feet as Charlie's garbled voice filled the room again, too high-pitched with pain. "Sabrina... Get her—"

Then, another gunshot fired, and the line went dead.

Chapter Nineteen

Sabrina sat in the living room in Tate's house, with the shades drawn and one lone light on, frustrated and worried and anxious for news.

According to officers Charlie Quinn and Max Becker, she hadn't been given the full details of the plan because they were need-to-know, and it was better if she really planned for a trip in case anyone was watching. Tate had never intended to take her on a weekend away, even a pretend one.

Pushing aside her frustration, Sabrina stood from the couch where she'd been sitting for over an hour, with nothing to entertain her but her thoughts.

Charlie wanted her to keep the television off since the house was supposed to appear empty and he didn't want to take any chances—a decision that had made Max roll his eyes and mutter something about "BS protection detail." But Charlie was the veteran so he'd won.

The two officers had been flipping through magazines in between walking around the small house and checking all the entry points. Sabrina had turned down the offers for their leftover police magazines and just waited.

After the way she and Tate had announced their plans all over town for the past few days, then flaunted that kiss in front of the hotel, she'd expected Adam to strike fast. As the time went by, she worried she might be here for days. And Tate had taken her weekend bag with him.

If she had to be here without him, she wanted to go upstairs and explore the rest of his house, see if it matched the easy comfort of the first floor. Tate had told her a lot about himself in the past few days, but he hadn't invited her into his home. Knowing it was probably the only chance she'd have to see it, she was tempted to explore. Instead, she walked over to the curtained windows.

"Please don't touch those," Charlie said, without looking up from his magazine.

"I was just—"

"If Adam followed you from the hotel to here and *didn't* fall for our ruse, we don't want to confirm anything."

He must have sensed her sudden apprehension, because he looked up and gave her a kind smile. "Don't worry. That's unlikely. But it's why we're here. And it's why we're keeping the shades down and most of the lights off. Just in case. Until we hear from Tate."

"I'm going to check in again," Max said, heading into the other room.

Sabrina strained to hear the conversation, but only the low rumble of Max's voice reached her.

When Max returned, all he said was, "No action."

She got the same update every hour for the rest of the day, until it got dark enough outside that even Charlie had given up on his magazines and was scrolling on his phone, periodically sighing.

"Maybe he's too smart to fall for this," Max suggested from the opposite side of the couch, where he'd settled an hour ago and had looked half-asleep ever since. "Or maybe he's moved on entirely, left Desparre and decided to find himself someone new to stalk."

Charlie scowled at his partner, then suggested to Sabrina, "Why don't you go upstairs? I saw a full bookshelf in Tate's second bedroom. I'm sure he wouldn't mind."

She debated only a few seconds, then hurried up the stairs. Lining the hallway were framed prints that looked like various nature scenes from Alaska. When she stepped closer to one, she saw it was labeled *Sitka, Alaska*. Wondering if he'd ever been there, if he'd loved the place enough to name his dog after it, she continued into the first room on the right.

Tate clearly used the room as his home office. There was a laptop open on a small desk against one wall, a pair of comfortable-looking chairs on another, and a bookshelf in between, overflowing with paperbacks. Smiling, Sabrina stepped closer, studying the titles in the light coming in from the hallway.

Tate had an affinity for historical nonfiction

and spy novels. He also had a whole section devoted to K-9 training. Even though he'd stuffed the shelves, he hadn't put anything on top of the bookshelf. She could picture her romance novels lining that space.

A wistful smile twitched, then dropped away, leaving behind an ache in her chest she didn't think would leave anytime soon.

The sudden boom from downstairs made her jump. Was that a gunshot?

For a brief moment, she felt paralyzed. Then she eased to the edge of the room, peering into the hallway. Should she go downstairs, look for Charlie and Max and stick close to them?

Boom! Boom! Boom!

A scream punctuated the final blast, and Sabrina raced into motion, scanning the room for something she could use as a weapon. Her heartbeat thundered in her ears, dimming the noise around her, but she still heard another anguished scream, followed by footsteps pounding up the stairs.

Spinning in a circle, Sabrina desperately looked for anything that might do some damage. But there was nothing except books and a laptop.

Hide! her mind screamed at her. Racing for the closet, Sabrina had just yanked open the door when a hand clamped on her shoulder.

A scream lodged in her throat, choking her, as she spun around, lifting her fists to fight back.

But it wasn't Adam. It was Max, with smears of blood across his cheeks and a look of horror in his eyes.

"Charlie?" she managed to ask, but he either didn't hear her or couldn't answer as he hustled her to the doorway, peeked out, then shoved her through it and across the hall into the bathroom.

"Get in. Lock the door." When she hesitated, wondering what he would do, he gave her a push. *"Now!"*

Shutting the door behind her, Sabrina fumbled with the lock, her hands shaking violently on the simple push mechanism. Someone could break through it easily.

Boom!

Sabrina shrieked at the gunshot, louder now, closer, and instinctively dropped to her knees in the dark bathroom.

Then the whole house seemed to fill with gunshots, and the sounds seemed to be all around her. She slapped her hands over her ears, blinking to try and see in the darkened room. Vague shapes took form—the bathtub, the toilet, a vanity—and she launched herself at the medicine cabinet.

She knocked her hand through it, searching for something useful, in the process dumping half the contents out. Then her hands closed around a straight razor. But what good would it do against a gun?

As another blast and then a loud thump sounded

from right outside the bathroom, Sabrina dropped the razor and grabbed the lid off the toilet tank. Standing just past the edge of where the door would open, she hefted it, ready to swing, even as she prayed Max would knock and tell her the threat was gone.

Instead, the door smashed inward with a loud thud, making Sabrina jump. It bounced against the wall, and then a hand caught it.

Sabrina lurched forward, raising the porcelain lid with shaky arms, hoping Adam would pause long enough at seeing her to let her get a swing in before he fired.

But it wasn't Adam who entered. It was someone shorter, but much more muscular. Someone decked out in dark fatigues, a ski mask over his face and a pistol in his hand.

In her surprise, she hesitated, and then his fist flew toward her, smashing into her face before she could jerk out of the way. The lid flew out of her hands, shattering as it hit the ground. She fell hard after it, the sight of Max's prone, bloodied form wavering at the edge of her vision before the world went dark.

Chapter Twenty

"What's going on?" Tate barked into the phone, sliding Sitka's vest on as Angie took the roads at dangerous speeds.

She was handling his vehicle like a pro, instead of a rookie who'd probably only done tactical driving at police academy.

"We're heading there now," Chief Griffith replied. "I don't have any updates. You know most of the officers were with you." His voice was dark and filled with self-blame as he said, "I didn't see this move coming."

Neither had Tate. In fact, Tate had thought this was the best way to keep Sabrina far away from any danger.

"Have Charlie or Max checked in?" If they had, the chief already would have told him, but Tate couldn't stop himself from asking the question. "Do we know if Sabrina is okay?"

"I don't know anything right now," the chief told him patiently. "Sam and I are on our way to your place. We closed up the station. I'll update you as soon as I can."

He hung up without another word, and Tate looked at Angie.

She didn't even glance his way, just hit the gas harder as Tate put his arms around Sitka to keep her from sliding around the truck. Then, mostly one-handed, he slid his own vest over his T-shirt, thankful that Angie had had the foresight to put hers on while he was trying to call Charlie back at the cabin.

Two other vehicles kept pace behind them, filled with the rest of the Desparre PD officers who'd been at the cabin to provide backup to him instead of watching Sabrina.

Frustration and anger built inside him until they burst out in a single curse.

"It's not your fault," Angie said, her voice high-pitched enough that he knew her outward calm was a facade. "This guy's a software engineer. Yeah, he's killed before, but I saw the report before I agreed to help. That murder was sloppy. He was going against a civilian, a marketing specialist with no reason to think he was in danger, not a pair of experienced officers."

How the hell had Adam gotten the jump on Charlie and Max?

Off the job, Tate was neutral on both of them. Max was the kind of guy who loved the power of the job, who didn't fraternize much with his fellow officers and wouldn't stick his neck out if you were in trouble with the brass. Charlie was a longtime veteran with strict ideas about who belonged on the force—and that hadn't included Tate's former partner, because Peter was hard of hearing. Still, if you were in danger on the job, both men would be there in an instant. In fact, they'd both risked their lives for him in the past. He respected them as officers.

He'd trusted them to watch over Sabrina without question. Even now, having heard the sheer amount of firepower Adam must have brought to the scene, Tate wasn't sure how Adam had gotten past both men.

Maybe he hadn't. The hope that refused to die was foolish, he knew. But he hung on to it as tightly as he could. Because ultimately, Adam's target wasn't Charlie or Max. It was Sabrina.

Stalkers who got to this level of obsession often killed their targets and anyone who stood in their way. But sometimes, they'd go a different route— abduction, assault.

Tate closed his eyes, wishing he didn't need to pray for the second choice. But at least she'd still be alive. At least he'd still have a chance to find her.

"We're close," Angie announced, and Tate opened his eyes, realizing he'd had them closed awhile, praying for Sabrina, Charlie and Max.

"All right," Tate said. "Let's—" He frowned as his phone buzzed with a text from the chief at the same time that an ambulance rounded the corner, coming from the direction of his house, sirens blaring.

They'd gotten help fast. The nearest hospital was an hour away, so they'd probably also gotten lucky, with medics happening to be nearby. It meant someone was still able to be saved. But who?

Tate's pulse rocketed as he opened the chief's text, hands shaking. But all it said was Scene is contained.

"Shit," Tate breathed. It was bad if the chief wasn't giving him news over text. The screen on his phone went blurry as tears flooded his vision. He blinked, swiping a hand over his eyes, and told himself it didn't mean Sabrina was dead.

It didn't mean all the impossible dreams he'd had about a real future with her were forever gone. It didn't mean the promises he'd made to her about getting her life back had been lies.

"We're here," Angie announced, slamming his truck to a stop and making Sitka yelp. "You good?"

"Yeah," Tate said, his hoarse voice marking him a liar. But even if the scene was contained, he still had a job to do. Justice to mete out.

Taking a deep breath, he tried to shove his fear and grief as deep as he could. Because being unfocused right now could get someone killed.

He stepped out of the truck, and Sitka leaped out beside him, moving one pace ahead of him as if she was trying to protect him from what he was about to see.

His house looked okay from the outside, except for the trail of blood leading down his front steps. His breath caught at the sight, then lodged painfully in his chest, and Tate faltered.

Before he could get moving again, the chief stepped outside. There was blood on his arms beneath the rolled-up sleeves of his uniform, and exhaustion and grief on his face.

As other vehicles slammed to a stop behind him and his fellow officers crowded around him to hear the news about their own, Tate stared at the chief. The air felt too heavy, too thick to get a solid breath, and his house wavered in front of him.

"Charlie was just rushed to the hospital," the chief said. "Max died at the scene."

A collective gasp behind him registered as the words hit Tate like a punch to the gut. No, he hadn't been personal friends with Max, but the man had put his life on the line for Sabrina. He was only a few years older than Tate, with a wife and two young sons at home.

"Sabrina is missing."

Tate blinked, trying to focus. Sabrina wasn't dead.

"There were at least two gunmen here today," the chief continued. "As Charlie was being loaded into the ambulance, he said they were wearing all black, looked like tactical gear. And black ski masks."

Tate swayed violently on his feet, an image in his mind of two masked men emerging from the trail parallel to him on a run five and a half years ago. Someone's hand—Angie's?—slapped his back and kept him upright as the chief demanded, "Talk to me, Emory. Could Adam have an accomplice?"

"It's not Adam," Tate breathed, a million regrets filling his mind.

He should have left Desparre the moment that news story had gone national, if not before then, when it had first been printed. He should have left Sabrina in the capable care of his fellow officers. Instead, he'd been selfish and stayed. That mistake had probably just cost Sabrina her life.

But not in a quick burst of gunfire like it might have happened if this were Adam. No, the officers who'd tried to kill him back in Boston were out for blood. His blood. And if they couldn't have it, they'd settle for making someone he loved suffer.

Chapter Twenty-One

Sabrina's head throbbed violently, shooting pain through her eyes as she tried to open them. Her mouth was cotton dry, and her hands and feet felt swollen and heavy.

She tried to move, tried to open her eyes. Panic flooded when she couldn't seem to do either, and her heart pounded frantically, almost painfully. Fear sent adrenaline shooting through her system, along with a realization of the last thing she'd seen.

Officer Max Becker lying in a pool of blood outside the bathroom door. A masked man standing over her, wielding a pistol. Then, the world had shifted and disappeared.

Was she still in Tate's house? Had the gunman left her for dead?

Swallowing back the sudden nausea, Sabrina forced her eyes open. The world in front of her swayed as it finally emerged from darkness.

She was lying awkwardly on her side on the floor. She definitely wasn't in Tate's bathroom or hallway but lying on dusty concrete. The world around her was dim, and she didn't think it was just her vision. The light seemed to be coming from certain areas only, the rest of the space in darkness. She could make out the wall across from her. It was concrete, too.

Where the hell was she?

Did Tate's house have a basement? Could she be down there? Or had the man taken her from Tate's house?

As she tried to push herself upright, her hands and feet caught, refusing to separate. The panic intensified, bringing tears to her eyes. She was bound at her wrists and ankles, tight enough that her hands and feet were partially asleep. Movement sent pins and needles pricking her nerve endings.

"She's awake."

The hard, emotionless statement made Sabrina jerk, searching for the source.

Booted feet stepped into view and she twisted, straining to see the face above her.

It wasn't covered by a mask anymore, yet she still didn't recognize him. Somehow, her abductor looked much taller than he had in Tate's bathroom. Lankier, too, with pale skin and reddish-blond hair. As he leaned toward her, she saw light blue eyes that didn't match her memory of hazel eyes behind the mask. He smirked at her and stood straight again as she tried to get her mouth to work.

"Whhhoare you?" she slurred.

"Get the camera," he called, and it took Sabrina a minute to realize he wasn't alone.

Another set of boots moved toward her, and as she twisted to look up at the person wearing them, she saw the hazel eyes from Tate's house. The man who'd knocked her out.

He was shorter than the first one by a solid nine inches, but he made up for it in bulk. His dark hair was sheared short, and his nose looked like it had been broken, probably more than once.

Hired guns Adam had found? It seemed more likely than him having made friends in Alaska who were willing to abduct someone for him.

The muscle-bound guy dragged a tripod across from her and set an old-fashioned video camera on it.

Dread dropped to her stomach as her fear multiplied and tears rushed to her eyes. What were they planning to do to her that they wanted to record?

Instinctively, she fought the bonds at her wrists and ankles, even though it just caused more pain.

The lanky one let out a harsh laugh and muttered, "No need. We'll take these off for you." The tone was so dark, it sent new fear through her.

"Who are you?" she managed, blinking until her vision cleared. "Why are you doing this?" Her voice came out stronger than she'd expected, sounded less afraid.

If Adam had sent them, why? Was he too much of a coward to hurt her himself?

"You picked the wrong man to shack up with," the lanky one said.

His accent registered as Bostonian, and Sabrina frowned, trying to understand. Did they think she'd *wanted* Adam to chase after her?

The bulky one snorted. "She doesn't get it," he told his friend.

His accent was also distinctly Boston. But none of the information Tate had shared about Adam's past mentioned him having lived there.

The lanky guy leaned close to her again, and Sabrina instinctively jerked back, wanting to get away.

"He didn't warn you, did he? He let you think he was some kind of stand-up guy, but the truth is he's a rat who's only loyal to himself." He gave her a crooked smile. "Sorry, honey, but you're going to pay for it."

"I didn't even know who he was until a week ago," she insisted, even though the dread building in her chest told her this wasn't about Adam at all.

The bulky guy shrugged, standing again. "When you found out, you should have run."

"Wouldn't have mattered," the lanky one put in. "He loves her, so it doesn't matter how she feels about him." Then he told his friend, "Get the ropes off. Camera is ready to go."

As his friend reached for her hands, Sabrina tried to wriggle away, but he yanked her arms upward, making her gasp at the sharp pain across her shoulders.

"Stay still." The blade of a knife slid too close to her wrists, and then her arms fell loose.

She wanted to wrench them in front of her, use them to claw at the guy's eyes while he was close to her, but they dropped uselessly, pain pricking like a thousand tiny pins.

How long had she been restrained and unconscious? How far away from Tate's house had they taken her?

The knife sliced again, this time through the bonds at her ankles, and then her feet were free, too. The sharp pains dancing across her feet at the sudden blood flow brought tears to her eyes.

"Get her up," the lanky guy said. "Remember, he'll probably take this to the cops, so no talking."

The bulky guy pulled her to her feet, but they were still asleep and wouldn't hold her. He grabbed her before she hit the ground, rolling his eyes as she tried to get her body to work.

She wiggled her toes and fingers, trying to get the blood flowing properly again, and just as she was starting to feel more stable, the guy let go. She swayed and fell backward against the cold concrete wall.

Glancing up, she saw more concrete above her. Where the hell was she?

The lanky guy stood across from her by the camera, against another wall. On either side of her, the space narrowed into what looked like hallways without doors to block the way. But there was only darkness, so she had no idea where either led.

"Let's do this," the bulky guy said, drawing her attention back to them as they both slid the masks over their faces again.

Panic struck. She knew she wouldn't make it, but she had to try. Shoving herself off the wall, she veered toward the hallway farther from the men, but her feet still weren't working properly, and the run she'd expected was an awkward stumble.

The lanky guy caught her easily and shoved her back into the wall.

She bounced off it, righting herself before she fell again.

"Sorry, honey. You sealed your own fate when you hooked your future to Tate Donnoly."

This was about *Tate*? The nonsensical words ran through her mind as she tried to process the wrong last name they'd used. Had they confused him with someone else?

Then the red light on the camera flashed on, and they both stepped purposely toward her.

Sabrina backed up, then she hit the wall again, and they were still coming. She threw her hands in front of her face, her mind whirling. Tate had grown up in the Midwest. He'd never mentioned Boston. But these men must have seen him picking her up at the hotel, dropping her at his house. They'd seen his face, so presumably they knew him.

"Please don't," she begged as they took another step closer and the lanky one smiled.

Panic overtook her, sending her heart rate into overdrive. "Tate doesn't care about me! It was all a setup. We're not really dating."

The bulky one snorted and then threw a punch that smashed into her cheekbone. It lifted her feet out from under her and made bright flashes of light strobe in front of her eyes.

She hit first the wall and then the ground, slamming into the hard concrete with a force that stole her breath. The sound seemed to echo in the hard-surfaced room, worsening her already-shaky equilibrium.

The other one swung a boot at her ribs, and she rolled, but not far or fast enough. It connected, sending new pain through her chest, and she curled into a ball, hoping to protect herself.

But one of them yanked her to her feet, only to hit her again, this time a punch to the other side of her face near her lips that made blood splatter across her face and fill her mouth. She flew backward, slamming into the wall.

Her head bounced against it, and her vision went dark, so she didn't see the next hit coming.

It landed under her chin, snapping her head back into the wall yet again. Her legs crumpled, and she threw her hands out to try and catch herself. Then, she hit the ground face-first, and the whole world blessedly disappeared.

"YOU'VE GOT SOME explaining to do," the chief told him, hands planted flat on Tate's kitchen table as he leaned over it toward Tate. "And I want the whole truth right now. No more lies. I need to know what we're dealing with here. I need to know *who* we're dealing with."

Noise from his fellow officers reached him from a distance. The officers were in the mudroom near his back entrance, dusting around the broken window where the assailants had entered. It was where Charlie had been found, facedown in a pool of blood, his hand still clutching his cracked cell phone.

Others were upstairs, dealing with evidence near where Max had been killed and Sabrina had been taken. Evidence of a struggle both inside and outside the bathroom suggested Max had locked her in there before he'd been killed defending her. The smashed lid from his toilet suggested Sabrina had grabbed the only available weapon and tried to defend herself. The blood on his bathroom floor said she'd paid for it.

"I'm sorry," Tate said, and his voice came out a pained whisper. "I never thought my past would catch up to me like this. If I had—"

The chief put up a hand. "We don't have time for regrets right now. What we need is a plan to move forward. So give me what I need to make an informed decision here, Emory."

Tate flinched at the use of his fake last name,

at all of the mistakes he'd made. If it could help save Sabrina, he'd gladly give up all of his secrets, even if it landed him in jail.

"My real name is Tate Donnoly."

The chief leaned back, as if pushed by the force of his surprise, then nodded for Tate to keep going.

"I was a police officer back in Boston before I came here. I was…able to create a fake name and start over in Alaska." He left out mention of his family friend in Witness Protection and the role his former chief had played, but the way Chief Griffith's eyes narrowed, he knew there was more to it.

"Back in Boston I witnessed three fellow officers taking a payoff from a crime lord. I reported it, and the whole situation was under investigation by the FBI when there was an attempt on my life." Tate blew out a heavy breath, remembering how close he'd come to dying that day. Jim Bellows, Kevin Fricker and Paul Martin were trained to take down an opponent fast and efficiently. He'd had the same training, but all Sabrina had was two years of running and trying to stay ahead of the threat against her.

Trying to focus, he told his chief, "The crime boss and one of the officers ultimately went to prison. But I never actually *saw* Kevin Fricker and Paul Martin try to kill me that day, only Jim, who fired the shot that hit me. And the FBI could only find a money trail to Jim. So Kevin and Paul got off. They stayed in the department until the stain got too bad, then went on to other departments. Other officers didn't trust them. They didn't trust me anymore, either. I knew that I'd gotten lucky and that Kevin and Paul might try again. Kevin made a threat on his last day, and I didn't want to risk my life or the people I loved so I took on a new name and started over here. Went through the academy again, came in as a Desparre PD rookie. I kept tabs on them over the years, but it seemed like I was safe here."

The chief nodded slowly, his gaze still assessing, probably seeing a lot more than Tate was saying. "Then that news article went national."

"Yeah," Tate agreed. "And we made a big show of how I fell for Sabrina."

Lines creased the chief's forehead, an understanding that since the Boston officers had gone after Sabrina instead of Tate, it meant they wanted to hurt her to get to him. "So what's their next step? Are we waiting for some kind of ransom note? A request to make a trade? You for Sabrina?"

"I sure hope so," Tate breathed. "But I think that's a best-case scenario. They blame me for all of it. Not just one of their closest friends going to jail and them being ousted from the Boston PD, but I cut off their second source of income—their payoff. Not to mention that I destroyed their reputations. They've hopped from one two-bit department to the next ever since."

"I'm not sure that's on you," Chief Griffith said. "Sounds like they may be doing it to themselves."

"But they blame me," Tate reiterated. "I thought if they ever came after me, it would be a bullet in the head in the middle of the night or maybe out on a remote call somewhere. But this…" He stared hard at the chief. "No matter what happens, Sabrina is the priority. I take responsibility for myself. If they want me, they can have me. Just please get her out." He glanced at Sitka, who whined and shuffled her feet, nudging him hard. His voice broke a little as he added, "And please take care of Sitka."

The chief nodded slowly. "You know civilians are always our priority. And we look after our own. Sitka is one of us."

From the front of the house, Officer Sam Jennings yelled, "We've got a delivery!"

Tate turned to run for the front yard when the chief added, "You're one of us, too, Tate."

He nodded his thanks, knowing how much of a show of faith that was, given how he'd lied and broken the law to get here. Then he hurried to where Sam stood, gingerly holding a manila envelope with gloved hands.

"How did it arrive?" the chief demanded from right behind Tate.

"Someone tossed it out of a van, then took off," Sam said. "Lorenzo and Nate went after him, but we all recognized the van. It's Old Oliver."

"Shit," Tate breathed. Old Oliver was Oliver Yardley, the dad of Young Oliver, who was equally eccentric. Old Oliver lived up in the mountain somewhere and periodically came into town and scared the newer locals with his long, untamed hair and beard and constantly darting eyes. He thought the government was spying on him, that anyone could be working for them, and even though the Desparre PD considered him generally harmless, half the time he didn't make much sense.

"Open it," the chief said.

"I got it," Tate said, grabbing the envelope from Sam. "After Paul left the Boston PD, he got training as a bomb tech at a different department." Ignoring the looks of confusion from his fellow officers, Tate walked far enough away that if it was a bomb, it wouldn't take out anyone else with him. "Stay!" he warned Sitka when she tried to follow.

She plopped onto her butt, but glanced up at his chief as if waiting for him to overrule Tate.

She whined when the chief ignored her, leaning forward as Tate took a deep breath and ripped open the envelope. What fell out wasn't a bomb but a flash drive.

Dread hit like a punch to his chest as he hurried wordlessly back inside and upstairs to his laptop. He tried not to see the huge bloodstain in his hallway, tried not to imagine Max's prone body there, but it didn't work.

He fit the flash drive into his computer, then braced himself as he felt the chief and several of his colleagues crowd behind him.

The audio came on first, Sabrina's terrified voice pleading, "Please don't!" Static covered most of her next words, but he heard his name. Then the video flashed on his screen, two men in all black partially blocking the camera as they stepped toward Sabrina. One of them laughed at her, then smashed a fist into her face.

Tate cringed, clenching his hands as she hit the floor hard and then got kicked in the ribs as she tried to roll away. They yanked her up, hit her twice more, sending blood flying before she crashed into the ground and didn't move.

Then the shorter, bulkier guy walked toward the camera, a self-satisfied smile showing through the mouth hole in his ski mask. Tate knew that smirk. Paul Martin.

Paul's hand reached toward the screen, showcasing bloody knuckles, before the video went dark.

A couple of the cops behind him swore, and the chief's hand clapped on Tate's shoulder as the camera flashed on again, this time facing the wall, where a piece of paper had been taped. Tate had to squint to read the sloppy, angry writing.

You did this to her. You want her pain to end? Go downtown and shoot yourself in the head. Otherwise, we'll get her back to you eventually. In pieces.

"We'll find her," the chief said softly as Tate's mind whirled and his stomach threatened to bring up the coffee he'd sipped at the cabin by the glacier.

"Old Oliver isn't giving us much," Lorenzo announced as he burst into the room. "He got paid to do it, says he doesn't know the guy who asked him to drop it off. We can pick him up again, but he's a dead end."

"Hey, I know that place," Nate said, pointing at the image frozen on the screen, all concrete around the single piece of paper.

Tate grabbed the young officer by his shoulders. Nate had grown up in Desparre, and he often complained that he'd run out of things to do here. "Where?"

Nate jerked slightly at the force of Tate's desperation. "It's an old army fort at the base of the mountain, near Luna. It's deserted and boarded up, but when I was a teenager, you could slip through the boards at the main entrance if you were thin enough. It used to be a place to go drinking."

"Let's go," Tate said, moving toward the door.

The chief stepped in his path. "We need a plan."

Tate stared him directly in the eyes. "I know these men, Chief. They're going to keep making tapes. They know I won't actually shoot myself, because *I know* they wouldn't let her go even if I did. But eventually, she won't be able to take any more." His voice broke, and he paused for a breath. "We need to hurry."

The chief nodded. "Okay. We'll plan on the way. Tate, you're with me. Sam, Lorenzo, Nate, you three follow." He turned to the final two officers present. "You two, continue securing the scene. And call the state PD or the FBI and tell them we need a bomb tech immediately. Don't stop calling until we get someone who will meet us there now."

Then the chief led Tate and Sitka down the stairs to his SUV, and the other officers followed on their tail. During the hour-long drive, the chief put the other officers on speaker, and they went over details.

According to Nate, there was only one entry point. "There is a maze of rooms in that fort," Nate insisted when Tate pressed him on it, "and I think at one point, there were multiple exits. Windows, too, but those have long since been closed up solid or collapsed. The actual entrances are all blocked off now or buried against the mountain and the forest that grew into it. There's only one way in."

The news made dread churn in Tate's gut. Kevin and Paul weren't the kind of guys to trap themselves anywhere. Did they think the fort was so out of the way, old and unused, that no one would recognize where they were? Or had they banked on Tate and his fellow officers recognizing it? Had they already moved somewhere else and left the single entrance rigged?

He shared his fears with the chief, who got back on the phone and confirmed the FBI bomb tech was already en route via helicopter and would probably beat them there.

They beat her, but only by five minutes. As soon as she arrived, she donned a massive bomb suit and waddled up to the boarded-up entrance of the fort.

"We've got a bomb," she confirmed grimly less than ten minutes later.

The entrance was set against the side of the mountain, hidden off an old, overgrown trail that seemed to lead nowhere now that the fort was defunct. The building was derelict, pieces of it crumbling around the entrance. The structure itself went on seemingly for miles, disappearing into the side of the mountain and within the forest that seemed to have swallowed most of it up.

"How long to defuse it?" the chief asked.

The bomb tech, a tiny Black woman with sharp eyes and sure fingers, shook her head. "Probably a couple hours."

Tate swore. Maybe that was Kevin and Paul's ultimate plan. Let him get here with enough time to save her but spend so long trying to get into the fort that it was too late. Because one thing he knew for sure: in a couple of hours, Sabrina would be dead.

Chapter Twenty-Two

The first thing Sabrina felt was an intense pounding in her head. It radiated down her neck and along her jaw. Even her eyes hurt.

She wanted to groan, but couldn't summon the energy. She cracked her eyes open, and they refused to go any farther. It wasn't exhaustion, she realized, but swelling.

Swallowing the moisture that had gathered in her mouth, she almost choked as she discovered it was blood.

The two men huddled across from her didn't seem to notice. They were arguing, their words echoing too loudly in her ears, intensifying the agony in her head.

Sabrina gently moved her jaw, trying to figure out if it was broken. New pain jolted up to her ears and down her neck, and tears blurred her vision.

Blinking them away, she looked down at herself. There was pain along her spine, and her hands and feet still throbbed. But she was still dressed, and no one had bothered to retie her bonds.

"What if he really *doesn't* care?" the bulky guy snapped.

"Relax, Paul," the lanky one replied. "You saw them at the hotel. He couldn't keep his hands off her. He'll come. And if he doesn't, we send another video." He shrugged. "Or we do what we threatened."

He glanced her way, and Sabrina closed her eyes, her heart thundering. But no footsteps sounded, at least not any she could hear over her pounding heartbeat and throbbing head. Finally, she eased her eyes open again. They weren't looking at her.

Paul's shoulders twitched, and there was discomfort on his face. "Or we just kill her. Drop her on his doorstep."

"Cops are there, moron," the lanky guy said.

"I didn't mean *literally*," Paul answered. "Geez, Kevin. But *I'm* not cutting her up. You want to do it, that's on you."

A shudder raced through Sabrina, violent and unstoppable, making her legs and arms twitch.

Both men glanced at her but immediately turned back to each other.

Her eyes were so swollen her captors couldn't tell they were open. The knowledge was only mildly comforting in the sea of panic swallowing her.

Her breathing hitched, threatening to make her choke on blood again, and Sabrina tried to tune out the men and focus on staying calm, on formulating some kind of plan. But she wasn't sure she could stand if she tried, and she certainly couldn't outrun them, even if she knew where to go.

Tears flooded again, and this time, she couldn't blink them away.

"You think Tate will recognize this place?" Paul asked, and Sabrina tried to focus again.

"If not, I'm sure one of the locals will. Stop second-guessing this. That local guide said the back entrance has been boarded up for a decade, and everyone knows it's impassable. There's no one out here to notice that we blew through those boards. We're good. They'll go to the main door, and they'll get themselves blown up."

Sabrina jerked at that, and Kevin looked her way, a slow smile on his face that told her he'd realized she was awake. Beyond enjoying her fear, he didn't seem to care, because he turned back to Paul and said, "Just relax. It'll all be over soon, and no one will ever know we were here." Then he pulled out his phone and focused on that.

Paul rolled his eyes, sank to the floor and leaned his head against the wall, staring upward.

Sabrina wiggled her toes in her shoes, bent her fingers. Her toes moved okay after a minute, but her fingers felt stiff and swollen, and she realized she'd thrown her hands up to block at least one blow. She'd probably taken a hit there. Or maybe she'd smashed them when she fell to the ground. She didn't remember falling again, but the ache across her face and chest and the way she was lying on her stomach, with her face twisted to the side, told her she had.

She needed a plan. Even if it was just to find her way to the door and blow it up herself before Tate could get there and trigger it. She didn't want to die like this, at the brutal fists of two men with some agenda she didn't understand. If this was the end, she wanted to go out fighting. Or at least saving the man she'd fallen for.

Trying to shift her body even slightly, maneuver her arms and hands out from underneath her, was surprisingly hard. It made new pain flash through her body and drew a groan she couldn't stifle.

The men barely spared her a glance, which told her she looked as bad as she felt. She kept trying, lifting her head to get a better look at her surroundings. Her neck made a terrible cracking sound, and the throbbing in her head amplified, obscuring her vision until she lowered her cheek down against the cold concrete.

Dizziness overwhelmed her, and she could feel herself being sucked under again. She tried to fight it, but the darkness claimed her.

IT HAD BEEN too long.

Tate shuffled from one foot to the other, watching the bomb tech—Njeri was her name—in her massive bomb suit meticulously working. He and the other officers were waiting at a distance.

The chief was continuously on the phone, digging up intel. He'd connected with Tate's old chief back in Boston, who'd been shocked to learn Tate had returned to Alaska and had expressed more worry than anger over Tate's illegal name change. Chief Griffith had also spoken with multiple police chiefs in Massachusetts who'd worked with Kevin and Paul. And he'd touched base with the officers handling the crime scene at Tate's house.

So far, he'd uncovered that a string of problems like unwarranted aggression and some suspected dirty dealing had followed Paul and Kevin from one department to the next. He'd found a general lack of surprise that they'd come after the man they'd apparently spent a lot of time railing against to their coworkers. But from their current departments, Chief Griffith's questions had been met with only careful statements that both men had taken personal time off. The chief had hung up those calls cursing about people covering their asses.

Tate's colleagues were on their own phones, following up on other connections the chief had dug up on his calls. Only Tate was left out of the work, since it seemed many of the people being contacted would either know him or know of him. Depending on what they'd heard from Kevin and Paul, that might not be good.

When the chief hung up his latest call and ran a hand over his eyes, Tate stepped closer to him. "There has to be another way in."

The chief shook his head. "Nate doesn't know

of one, and he knows the mountains of Desparre better than any of us. I called the park service. They say normally this place might have become a tourist attraction, but the remote location and the fact that there are health concerns with it has kept it boarded up and off-limits. The fort originally had at least three entrances. One of those caved in a long time ago. The other was boarded up ages ago, but it might still be accessible. Unfortunately, they don't know where it is because the fort has been defunct since the end of World War II. The forest grew in around it. They're tracking down some local guides and are supposed to get back to me."

"I'm going to see if Sitka can sniff anything out."

At the sound of her name, Sitka jumped to her feet. She ran a tight circle around him, wagging her tail.

The chief glanced from him to Sitka, then back again. He nodded slowly. "Okay. Just keep me in the loop—and I mean every fifteen minutes, Tate. If you weren't Sitka's handler, I'd send someone else with her right now. As it is, I need the rest of my team here, ready to go as soon as the bomb is defused. Njeri is making faster progress than she'd initially thought."

Tate nodded, then walked Sitka up next to Njeri.

She spun to face him and demanded, "What the *hell* are you doing?"

"We just need a quick sniff," he answered as Sitka put her nose to the thick layers of wood nailed across the entrance. Whatever gap had existed when Nate was a teenager had apparently been boarded over, because there was barely enough room for air to pass through now.

The boards looked relatively new, but whether Paul and Kevin had nailed them in place themselves after trapping Sabrina in there and rigging the place or whether someone had done so years ago, Tate wasn't sure. The only thing he knew was that if the crooked cops were still inside, they would have had to go in another way.

Sitka sniffed a line across the boards, then her nose came up. She sniffed the air and started moving around the side of the building. Tate followed, with Njeri's curse trailing after him.

Sitka stuck to the edge of the building as it disappeared into thicker woods, until Tate could no longer see his fellow officers. Then she veered right, away from the mountain, and started running.

Tate hesitated, then ran after her. She'd been right when they'd searched the woods behind Sabrina's house. He had to believe she could do it this time, too.

Hold on, Sabrina, he willed her, as his hand instinctively rested on his pistol. Besides the Taser and pepper spray, it was his only weapon. He had no doubt that Paul and Kevin had more. Hopefully, he wouldn't come across them too abruptly and be forced into a firefight before he could get backup.

As the forest closed in around him and Sitka, she slowed on a trail big enough to hold a four-wheeler and then veered left. Tate unsnapped the top of his holster. Last fall's dead leaves crunched under his feet, but he couldn't hear his fellow officers anymore even if he strained. All he could hear was Sitka's sure footsteps as she raced forward, leaping over a fallen log.

Tate ran around it, trying to keep up. He almost went down as his feet slid across a pile of smaller sticks on the other side, and then his breath caught. Up ahead was more of the fort, emerging from the mountain and surrounded by debris that looked like pieces of plywood, broken and splintered. Beyond it, possibly…a door?

Sitka turned her head toward him, and before she could bark, Tate put his hand to his lips and whispered, "Sitka, quiet."

She complied, her tail wagging frantically.

His pulse doubled as he crept forward. When he glanced down, he realized he'd pulled his weapon out without conscious thought.

After a few more steps, he was certain. Sitka had found the other entrance.

It was no longer boarded up. Apparently, Kevin and Paul had blasted their way inside with another bomb. Now it was a clear entrance they'd probably assumed no one would find.

Tears rushed to his eyes as he stepped up next to his dog, petted her head and praised her. "Good girl!"

She thumped her tail, and he urged her over to the side, around the corner from the door, in case Paul or Kevin stepped outside. Then he pulled out his cell phone and sent the chief a quick text about where he was, hoping the chief would be able to follow his directions.

Tucking his phone away, he glanced back the way they'd come. He tried to gauge how long it would take for his fellow officers to get here. His stomach churned at the delay, especially as his mind put Sabrina's beating on replay.

"Stay with me, girl," he told Sitka. "We're going to work."

From somewhere inside the cavernous fort, a voice echoed. "I think it's time to cut our losses and get out before they find us. Let's kill her now."

He recognized that voice. Paul Martin.

Saying a quick prayer, Tate stepped inside. Sitka slipped in next to him.

After the bright sunshine outside, his eyes took a minute to adjust to the long, dark hallway. It smelled dank and stuffy, like no one had used it since World War II.

He tried to will his heartbeat to normalize, to

treat this like any other police callout. But this wasn't like any call he'd ever been to. This was Sabrina.

As his eyes started to adjust, Tate slipped his finger alongside the trigger. He raised his weapon and slid along the wall, toward the sound of Paul's voice. Sitka stuck right on his heels.

"Don't wimp out on me now." Kevin's voice reached him. "Don't you want to hear the explosion?"

Paul's response was muttered and sounded like a curse.

Beside him, Tate could feel more than see the fur on Sitka's back rise as there was a thump, and then Sabrina groaned in pain.

His whole body tensed with anger and shared pain, and then he was standing next to an open doorway. Gesturing for Sitka to ease in beside him where she wouldn't be seen, Tate peeked carefully around the corner.

Kevin was leaning against the wall diagonal from him, standing near a tripod as he scrolled on his phone. There was a pistol tucked into the waistband of his black pants and a length of rope near his feet.

Tate heard Paul from the opposite wall, muttering. He was pretty sure Sabrina was over that way, too.

Lowering himself slowly, silently to the floor while Sitka remained motionless beside him, Tate edged millimeter by millimeter until he could see around the corner.

Paul stood next to Sabrina's prone form, his hands fisted and his gun within easy reach at his waist. There was a foldable knife clipped to his waistband, too.

Sabrina was lying on her stomach, her arms tucked underneath her. Her legs were curled slightly inward protectively, her neck twisted so she wasn't facedown. There was dried blood caked to her lips and chin, and her eyes were swollen and bruised.

The sight made nausea and fury mingle in his belly. He might not have thrown the blows, but this was his fault.

Focus, he reminded himself. Forcing his gaze off her, Tate darted one more look toward Kevin, who was still on his phone, seemingly oblivious to Paul's fury. Then he slid carefully backward.

There was no good way in.

Kevin and Paul were too far apart. Even if he sent Sitka after Paul while he shot Kevin, it would be dicey getting through the doorway fast enough. Paul and Kevin might have time to pull their weapons, especially Kevin, who had one of the fastest draws Tate had ever seen.

Was his team close? Risking a glance at his phone, he saw that he had no bars. The text he'd sent the chief was marked Unable to send.

A curse built inside him, along with new fear.

Did he turn back? Risk the chance of them hearing his retreat? Risk them deciding to get rid of Sabrina before he could make the trek to his team and back?

His pulse thundered as sweat slicked his hands. There was really no decision. He had one chance to get this right.

But if he and Sitka were even the slightest bit off their marks, Sabrina would be the first to die.

Chapter Twenty-Three

"They're here!"

Paul's shout roused her. It took all of Sabrina's energy to force her eyes open again. This time, she could see even less. Just a sliver of the room, partially obscured by her eyelashes.

It seemed like Paul had just stepped over to the doorway on the left a second ago, but now he was moving toward her again, a nervous grin twitching on his face. "They're trying to defuse the bomb."

Hope blossomed beneath her pain until he added, "It'll happen soon. They'll think they've got the bomb defused and trigger the secondary device."

Fear erupted, overriding her pain, and Sabrina tried to stare down the long hallway, estimate how far it was to the door. But she could only see the first few feet, lit up by a lantern they'd set at the edge of the room. Beyond that was darkness. And she wasn't sure she could stand up, let alone run to the door before they caught her.

If Tate and his teammates were already working on the door, her trying to set off the bomb wouldn't save them, anyway. It would kill everyone.

Frustration tensed her chest, sent a new wave of pain through her body that she ignored. She refused to lie here and wait to die. But what options did she have?

She sucked in a deep breath, trying to clear the haze in her mind as well as give her body strength. The faint scent of dog and sandalwood filled her nose, and she couldn't stop her loud exhale, which sounded like something between laughter and a cry. She must be in bad shape if she was hallucinating Tate and Sitka nearby.

Kevin glanced her way, but she didn't hold his interest long before he was back on his phone, muttering to himself, "Soon, soon." Then he paused and glanced at Paul. "You sure we're safe here?" He looked up at the ceiling, which had crumbled in places and was stained from years of neglect and moisture. "I'm not sure how structurally sound this place is."

Paul grinned, seeming suddenly in his element. "We're fine. This fort has been standing since World War II. Besides, it's a directed charge. It'll blow out, not toward us. While they're cleaning up body parts—assuming anyone was standing far enough back not to get hit—we'll go out the back way."

Kevin nodded as he pushed away from the wall, tucked his phone in his pocket. He looked a lot more alert, anticipatory.

Sabrina took another deep breath, and the imaginary scents were gone. She wedged her hand underneath her chest and shifted slightly, getting a better angle for her neck. Then her breath caught and her eyes widened enough to realize she wasn't hallucinating.

That was Tate's head she'd just seen disappearing around the corner, down low, on the ground like her.

Hope and fear mingled, made her heart race. But as her gaze swept Paul and Kevin, she realized there was no good way into the room, even if Tate had a lot of backup.

She thought back over the almost two weeks she'd spent stuck in that hotel room, the times Tate had stopped by and they'd talked about anything and everything. He'd given her some insight into how police officers worked, the precautions and the dangers.

Something that had stuck out to her then because she'd never considered it was the danger of doorways. It made you exposed, gave a prepared criminal an easy spot to focus their weapons on and just wait. If you had to go in, you moved fast and got out of the doorway immediately.

If that was Tate's plan, who was with him? Only one officer could fit through the doorway at a time, and Kevin and Paul were at opposite sides of the room, Paul having taken up his typical spot near her.

They might not know Tate was here, but since Paul's announcement that officers were working to get past the bomb, they were alert. Kevin's hand had settled on his gun, and he kept licking his lips, like he couldn't wait to use it on someone. Paul was pacing back and forth, and he'd pulled his knife out, kept flicking it. Open, closed, open, closed.

If Tate came through that doorway, even if he had the element of surprise, could he really take out both Paul and Kevin before one of them killed him? Or her?

Fear cramped her stomach and tunneled her vision, and she closed her eyes, tried to think. She needed to help. She needed a way to distract them.

Hoping to clear her mind again, she took a deep breath and gagged on something, maybe even more of her own blood. She tried to breathe through it, but it just got worse, choking her as she erupted in a fit of coughing.

"Get her up," Kevin snapped from what seemed like far away. "We might need her. Don't let her choke."

Paul gave a loud sigh, then tucked his knife back into his waistband. Then he stepped closer, grabbed her arms roughly and flipped her to her back.

It only made the coughing worse, and she tried to lean forward to get some air as he dragged her toward the wall. Tears obscured her vision and ran down her face as he propped her against the wall, then started to straighten.

This was it. This was her chance.

Fighting through the coughing that wouldn't stop, Sabrina lunged toward him, blinking back tears as she made a grab for the gun at his waistband.

"HEY!" PAUL YELLED, startling Tate as he climbed to his feet.

He peered around the corner and saw Kevin, wide-eyed and pulling his gun from his waistband.

From the other side of the room, he heard a scuffling, then a thump and Sabrina's yelp of pain.

He'd run out of time.

"Sitka, go get!" he commanded. Then he lifted his weapon and lunged into the room, breaking right.

Kevin already had his weapon up toward Sabrina, but at Tate's entrance, he swiveled, redirecting it at Tate.

Tate slid his finger under the trigger guard, his heart thundering, his breathing erratic, his movements desperate. Kevin was one of the best shooters he'd ever seen. He was fast, too fast.

From his peripheral vision, Tate saw a blur of fur and lean muscles as Sitka raced past him, then launched herself into the air, straight at Paul.

Tate fired, and the blast of his bullet leaving the

chamber echoed and echoed. Too late he realized it wasn't just his own bullet sounding.

His left arm screamed in agony as he flew backward, landing hard on the concrete floor, then sliding into the wall with a dull thud. *A matching scar for the other side.*

To his left, Sitka slammed into Paul, knocking the muscle-bound man to the floor. His gun, which Tate suddenly realized had been in a tug-of-war between Paul and Sabrina, skidded toward Tate.

Sitka shook her head, biting down hard on Paul's arm as the man screamed and twisted, trying to get away.

Ignoring the blood sliding down his left arm, Tate lifted his gun again. His right hand shook as he redirected at Kevin, who'd taken a bullet, too.

It had slammed the man into the wall, but he was recovering faster than Tate, even though Tate could have sworn his bullet had headed for center mass.

He had a vest on, Tate realized as Kevin swung his gun up again, too, hatred in his eyes.

Wasting precious seconds to lift his arm higher, up from center mass where he'd been trained to shoot, Tate fired again, once, twice.

Kevin's eyes widened as a cloud of blood erupted from his neck. He slid down the wall, his gun hitting the floor first.

From the opposite direction of where Tate had

entered, a distant *bang, bang, bang* sounded. The sound of a battering ram. His colleagues were coming, breaking through the boards at the entrance. They must have gotten the bomb defused faster than expected.

Pivoting back toward Paul, Sitka and Sabrina, Tate swore and shoved to his feet.

Paul had yanked the knife off his waistband. As Sabrina launched herself toward Paul's gun, groaning as she slammed into the concrete again, Paul flicked the knife open.

He lifted his hand back to drive it into Sitka.

Sitka kept shaking her head, biting down harder, ignoring the threat and never giving up on her target as the knife arced toward her.

Tate didn't have a shot. Sliding the gun back into his belt, he jumped forward, praying his vest would take the stab if he misjudged his aim.

He landed hard, smacking against Sitka and making her yelp. But she still didn't let go.

His injured arm screamed in protest, sending spikes of pain through his head. He twisted, trying to get a hold of Paul's knife, which had been pushed backward at the force of Tate's landing.

Then the knife was up again, coming for Tate's bad arm. The arm he couldn't move well enough or fast enough to block it.

He gritted his teeth, preparing for the pain even as he fought for a grip on the man's arm. He grabbed hold with both hands just below the elbow, his arms shaking as he tried to keep the knife at bay.

Paul's overly bulky muscle wasn't for show. The man was *strong*. He let out a deep, sustained yell as Sitka kept biting, kept shaking him, but still he forced the knife downward, changing direction so he was aiming for Tate's face.

Then he slammed his forehead into the side of Tate's head, letting out another scream as he made contact.

Tate's head bounced sideways with a crack, and his grip loosened.

The knife surged toward him, nicking a line across his cheek before he regained his hold.

Sitka growled low and deep, and Tate let out his own yell as he forced his injured arm to work harder, pushing the knife away.

From a distance, footsteps pounded toward them, but the knife was moving forward again, and Tate's injured arm started violently shaking.

"Drop it. *Now!*" The voice was weak, but the tone was deadly serious.

Tate's gaze jerked up to where Sabrina stood, swaying on her feet, blood dripping from her face. Paul's gun shook in her hands, but she had it angled well, lined up with Paul's face through the gap behind Tate.

Paul's gaze darted from her to Kevin and back again.

Tate took advantage of his momentary distraction to launch sideways, using his weight on Paul's arm as he grabbed the man's wrist and twisted.

Paul yelped, his muscles engaging too late as the knife clattered to the ground.

Tate kicked it aside and pushed to his feet.

Then his colleagues rushed the room, and Tate told Sitka, "Let go!"

She opened her jaw and dropped Paul's arm, then moved out of the way, letting the other officers do their jobs.

Tate could only stare at Sabrina. She'd dropped her arm to the side, but she still held the weapon. She stared back at him through badly swollen eyes, and a wave of intense relief and residual terror and realization washed over him.

She was alive.

She blinked a few times, then the gun clattered to the floor, and she collapsed.

Rushing forward, Tate caught her before she landed. His arm gave out, and he slid to his knees, trying to take her weight.

"Get an ambulance." The chief's voice rang in Tate's ears as he fumbled to see Sabrina's face, to check her breathing.

Arm shaking, he managed to get a hand on her neck and feel for a pulse. Tears rushed to his eyes when he found one.

Then the chief warned him not to move her.

"She probably has internal bleeding. We'll get the medevac."

They were closer to Luna and the hospital than they would have been back in Desparre, but they were deep in the woods, in the bowels of an old fort. A helicopter couldn't land here.

Fear once again gripped him. Had he gotten to her in time, only to lose her anyway?

Chapter Twenty-Four

It had been almost thirty-six hours since Kevin had been declared dead at the scene and Paul had been taken into custody. Not only had the Desparre police defused the bomb he'd built, but apparently the secondary device Njeri had spotted was something Paul had trained on only the month before. They were already building a rock-solid case against him. The chief thought maybe this time they'd dig deep enough to find the money they hadn't located the first time around. Paul was unlikely to ever again step outside a prison.

Tate blinked at his watch, then rubbed sleep from his eyes and leaned over to pet Sitka, who was snoring on the hospital floor. Technically, she wasn't supposed to be here, but she was a police K-9, so they'd made an exception.

His left arm ached at the movement, but it was dulled by the painkillers they'd given him after they'd stitched him up. The bullet had passed through the muscle in his biceps and gone out the other side. He'd need physical therapy, just like last time, but he would recover. And the plastic surgeon who'd closed up the cut on his face had told him he probably wouldn't have a scar.

In the hospital bed, Sabrina twitched and then let out a whimper in her sleep.

He leaned toward her from the chair the hospital staff had pulled in, along with coffee for him and a bowl of water for Sitka. Once they'd gotten Sabrina into a room, he hadn't left her side.

But she still hadn't woken up. As soon as she'd arrived at the hospital, doctors had rushed her in for CT scans of her brain, facial bones, neck, abdomen and pelvis. She'd been wheeled away from him, looking small and battered and helpless in that hospital bed, a far cry from the determined woman who'd stood, blood-covered and swaying, and saved his life.

At the time, overhearing snippets of the doctors' conversations, phrases like *check for a fractured skull* and *could have an intracranial hemorrhage* had terrified him. They'd gotten him stitched up only by assuring him they'd tell him if there were any changes to or any news on Sabrina's condition.

Hours later, they'd told him either she was very lucky or her assailants had known exactly how to hit to cause a lot of visual damage but not to kill her. They said she had a couple of fractured ribs that luckily hadn't punctured her lungs. But she had a lung contusion that would need pain management. Amazingly, despite the massive swelling and bleeding on her face, she hadn't broken any of the bones there. But she did have a brain contusion. The doctors had called it minor, said the microbleed would require a longer stay in the hospital. It was also what was keeping her unconscious.

She was medicated, needed time to heal, but every moment her eyes stayed closed made him more anxious. Her doctors planned to keep her in the hospital for at least a week but said she would most likely make a full recovery within six months. But *most likely* wasn't good enough.

Somehow, in the time he'd spent with her at her hotel room and pretending to be her boyfriend, he'd fallen for her for real. Or maybe it had happened long before that, when she'd first come to the police station asking for help. Or even before that, when he'd run into her in town and felt an instant connection he wanted to pursue.

"Tate."

The whisper came from the doorway of Sabrina's room. After giving her one more glance to be sure she wasn't waking, Tate forced himself to his feet. His whole body ached as he hobbled toward his chief.

"How's she doing?"

"Nothing new," Tate told him. His fellow officers hadn't left the hospital until a few hours ago, exhausted. Luna police had taken over, stationing an officer at each of the two hospital entrances to protect both him and Sabrina. At this point, they all assumed Adam had left, that finding him would become a longer-term investigation. But they weren't taking any chances.

Tate hadn't realized his chief had stayed.

"I've got an update on Charlie."

Worry clamped down on his chest until the chief said, "The surgery was a success. They stopped the internal bleeding. He's got a lot of healing ahead, but he's going to make it."

Tate let out a relieved breath.

"And so are you."

When Tate shook his head, not understanding, the chief said, "The two of us have a lot of paperwork ahead, getting your personnel file in order. And there's a suspension in your future because I can't just pretend this didn't happen. But obviously, the threat against you was real. So, I'm willing to accept that you did what you had to do."

Relief loosened the tension he hadn't even realized he'd felt underneath his worry for Sabrina. "Thank you."

"You're a good officer, Tate. We want to keep you." He held out his hand as Sitka jerked upright, then ran over.

Tate shook his hand, then the chief bent over and petted Sitka. "You, too. You make one hell of a K-9 unit."

She gave the chief's arm a slobbery kiss, and he smiled, then stood.

He turned to leave, then twisted back toward Tate. "Don't give up," he advised, nodding toward Sabrina.

"Doctors said—"

"I know what the doctors said," the chief interrupted. "I'm talking about you. Don't give up on her. Believe me when I say I know what I'm talking about." Something wistful and sad flashed over his face as he said, "This kind of connection doesn't come around often. When you find it, hang on as long as you can."

"Thanks," Tate replied when he finally found his voice. By then, the chief was already striding away.

He glanced down at Sitka, who looked from him to Sabrina.

Tate's gaze followed, then he jerked in surprise. Her eyes were open, staring at him. She looked groggy, but far more aware than he would have expected after all she'd been through.

Rushing back into the room, with Sitka keeping pace, he carefully took hold of her hand. "How are you feeling?"

"Like a couple of assholes beat me up," she rasped.

Relief made his laughter come out sounding like a half sob. He stroked his thumb over the skin on her hand, mottled purple with bruises. "You're going to be fine."

The words seemed to reassure her, but her eyes closed again. They didn't open again for several long minutes. When they finally did, a nurse came in and listened to her heartbeat, then checked her pupils and helped her sit.

She gave Sabrina some water, then patted her arm, above where Tate still held her hand. "I know you don't feel so great now, but you'll be all right. You press your call button if you need me, okay?"

When Sabrina gave a shaky nod, looking a lot more alert, the nurse smiled at both of them, then left them alone.

Sabrina stared at the open doorway for a long moment. Then her lips pursed, lines forming between her eyes as she turned back to him, her expression one of wariness and distrust. "Who were they? Why were they trying to get back at you?" Her tone turned accusatory as she demanded, "And why did they call you Tate *Donnoly*?"

"I'm sorry." His voice came out barely more than a whisper, so he cleared his throat and tried again. "I'm sorry." He gave her the short version of the attempt on his life and his subsequent name change and return to Alaska.

Her gaze shifted to Sitka. "You didn't grow up in the Midwest." She looked back at him. "You grew up in Sitka, Alaska, didn't you?"

His dog let out a soft woof, then laid her head on the edge of Sabrina's hospital bed.

"Yes."

"You lied to me."

"I had to. I was trying to keep you safe. I was

trying to keep *everyone* safe. I swear to you, Sabrina, I thought that article had gone unnoticed. Just in case, I was planning to leave after I helped you find your stalker. If I thought there was an immediate threat, I never would have—"

"You dug into my life without my permission," she cut him off. "And I get it. You did it to help me. But I told you *everything* afterward. I was really honest with you. Not just about what happened but about my *life*. About my family and my friends and who I really am. The whole time you were lying to me."

He clamped his lips shut as she spoke, letting her talk. But then he couldn't keep quiet anymore. "I tried to be honest with you."

She let out a huff. "When?"

"With everything. I told you more about myself than I've shared with anyone since I left Boston. Yes, I hid some of the small details that I thought were dangerous for you to know—like the fact that I used to be a cop in Boston, that I'd grown up in Alaska. But the rest of it? All the things I shared with you about my family and my dreams for my life? That was all true."

"The things you left out weren't small details," Sabrina said, her voice too calm now, like she was tired of it all. Tired of him. "You hid pretty important pieces of yourself. Including a threat. And I paid for it."

"I know." He slid his hand over hers, and she frowned, pulling her hand free.

Dread built up, the fear that he'd messed up so badly there was no coming back from it. But the chief was right. He had to try.

"I'm so sorry, Sabrina. I can't take that back. If I had suspected what would happen, I would have left."

She flinched a little at that, and it gave him hope.

He leaned closer and stared into her eyes, hoping she could see the truth there. "I love you, Sabrina."

Her lips parted as she stared back at him. Then tears welled up, and she blinked them away. Her voice was a whisper when she said, "I don't think I can forgive you."

SABRINA WOKE WITH a start, her heart thundering in her chest, her head and ribs aching. She blinked, trying to get her bearings.

She was in a dark hospital room. Not a hidden concrete fort, trapped in by crooked cops, thinking her only option was how she might die. By bullet, beating or bomb.

Taking a deep breath, she glanced around. Tate was asleep in a chair across from her bed. When she strained, she spotted Sitka sprawled at his feet, lightly snoring.

She didn't remember drifting off to sleep again,

but the stiffness in her body that turned into sharp pain at any movement, told her it might have been a while. She did remember the doctor coming in, giving her a whole lot of medical speak that had made her head spin, then summing up with "You'll be okay. Your brain and your ribs need time to heal, but you'll get there."

Then she'd been alone with Tate again, struggling to figure out what else to say. He'd told her he *loved* her. But it didn't matter how she felt in return, not if she couldn't trust him.

He'd hidden his past from her. Hidden the threats against him. After she'd spent two years running from a stalker, he should have known how much of a difference the right information could make. Instead, he'd left her in the dark, clueless about the additional danger she faced.

Her fists clenched, and the movement tugged on her IV, stinging. But the pain was a welcome distraction from her building anger.

If he'd been totally honest with her, maybe she wouldn't have done anything different. Maybe she would have felt the same way he had about the likelihood of his past coming to get her. But at least then she wouldn't have this sense of betrayal that hurt worse than all of her injuries combined.

She loved him.

The realization hit with the force of one of the punches she'd taken to the head. She huffed out a humorless laugh, and her chest started to ache.

How hadn't she realized it earlier? Of course she'd fallen in love with Tate, no matter his last name. He was sweet and smart and funny, and all the struggles of the past few years had seemed lighter when she was with him.

When Jessamyn had joked that maybe she'd meet her soul mate in that bar two and a half years ago and Sabrina had rolled her eyes, she'd thought about how her married friends liked to tell her that when she met the right one she'd just *know*. Adam had spotted her in that bar, begun his unnatural obsession that had led her to Desparre. That had led her to Tate. And now, suddenly, she *knew*.

But did that matter if she couldn't trust him?

Squeezing her eyes closed, she tried to imagine going home and never seeing him again. The idea was painful, and she didn't want to face it. When she opened her eyes again, a silhouette in the open doorway made her jump.

She almost didn't recognize him, with his hair dyed darker, the glasses, and the hospital scrubs. Obviously the Luna cops watching the entrances hadn't recognized him. But when he stepped inside, there was no doubt.

Fear mingled with a deep sense of betrayal. Adam had spent more than two years destroying her life, then convinced her to see him as a friend.

Adam smiled with a darkness in his eyes as he put a finger to his lips. Then he twisted toward Tate, his expression shifting into a possessive fury. His arm twitched, drawing her attention to what he held. A gun.

Sabrina's gaze went from him to Tate, asleep on the chair.

She didn't think. She just leaped.

The IV ripped out of her hand, and her bruised ribs set off a ferocious, searing pain that nauseated her. Her head jostled, and it felt as if her brain was bouncing inside her skull.

Then everything seemed to happen at once.

She smashed into Adam, propelling him back and pushing the gun sideways. Adam's gaze locked on hers, a mix of jealous rage and sinister intent that sent goose bumps across her neck. Then his hands shifted, ready to shove her back.

Before he could move, Tate jumped out of his seat, awakened by the noise. He knocked over his chair as he pushed his way between them, smashing Adam's gun hand into the wall, and making him drop the weapon.

Then somehow, Sitka was there, pressed up against her when she might have swayed and fallen.

Tate spun Adam face-first into the wall, yanked handcuffs off his belt and slapped them on as nurses and doctors rushed toward them and Tate told them to call for backup.

"She's mine," Adam snarled, trying to twist out of Tate's grip.

Tate pushed him back into the wall as he turned his head to look at her. "You okay?"

She stared back at him, at the intense protectiveness in his eyes, at the love she could see there.

The love she felt in return made her chest ache, made the words want to burst free.

Instead, she managed to nod as tears filled her eyes. She gave him a shaky smile to reassure him she really was okay and that she hadn't reinjured herself badly.

When Sitka whined, Sabrina stroked her fur, still staring at Tate. She didn't take her gaze off him, even when a pair of officers rushed into the room and pulled Adam away.

It was over.

After two long years of running and hiding and thinking she'd never have her life back, they'd caught her stalker. She could go home, return to the life she'd made for herself there.

So, why did her chest suddenly ache so badly over all the things she was giving up in Alaska?

Epilogue

Sabrina pulled back the curtains on her living room window, exposing the glorious view she'd fallen in love with the moment she'd stepped foot in this cabin.

She took a deep breath, smiling when her ribs gave only a slight twinge in protest. She'd spent a full week in the hospital, while doctors gave her medication to help her manage the pain and tests to check her neurological state. Then they'd declared the small bleed in her head healed enough to release her.

For the next three months at least, they'd told her to expect her symptoms to persist. Ringing in her ears maybe or some dizziness or just not feeling quite right. They wanted her to have regular follow-ups with a neurologist back in New York. But they'd cleared her to travel.

Her bags were already packed. She'd left New York two years ago with a trunk full of belongings. She was returning with two duffel bags.

But she was also returning with a feeling of safety. Adam was in custody. He had admitted to killing Dylan. He'd admitted to setting the truck on Sitka. He'd even admitted to giving her a shove in the woods, then grabbing her arm to ostensibly save her.

Apparently, he'd searched for her for over a

year and a half without success after she'd left New York. Then she'd started her online jewelry business. She didn't remember it, but years ago, she'd posted something on social media about her dreams of designing jewelry, even shared a drawing of a necklace. A friend had shared that post. Then in Alaska, Sabrina had finally made that necklace. Adam had spent so much time obsessively trying to trace her online that the single post had eventually led him to her, through the PO box she used when she mailed out the jewelry.

She shivered at the deviousness, the obsessiveness he'd demonstrated. But it was over now. She straightened, pushing Adam from her mind as she looked around the place she'd come to call home.

She was going to miss this cabin. She was going to miss this town, miss the people.

A familiar pain clamped down on her chest, and she pressed a hand against her heart. After Adam had been arrested, she'd told Tate to go home, that she needed time. She knew how she felt about him, but she didn't know if she could do anything about it.

She hadn't told him she loved him. She wasn't sure she ever would. But meeting him and Sitka, coming to love him and Sitka, made leaving Alaska painful.

Glancing around the cabin one more time, she reached for her duffel bags. Lifting them sent a searing pain across her ribs and caused her head to swim. She closed her eyes and breathed through the pain until it eased up. Then she moved slowly toward the door.

No matter what she decided, she'd call Tate once she got to New York. She'd debated stopping by his house on her way to the airport, but worried if she did, she'd break down. She wanted time to feel more whole, to have more distance from the attacks in the army fort, before making any big decisions about her future.

She might come back here someday. Might see Tate and Sitka again. But maybe they both needed to return to the lives they'd left behind before they could decide what their futures held.

Pulling the door open, she drew in a hard breath. "Tate."

He stood on her porch, his hands twisted together like he'd been wringing them. He looked serious and determined and exactly what her eyes wanted to see.

Woof!

A smile trembled on her lips as she looked to his side, at the beautiful dog. "Sitka."

"I know you wanted time," he said, his gaze going to the bags she carried. His lips tightened briefly, then his gaze returned to hers. "But I just needed you to know something."

Sabrina nodded slowly as she took a step backward, never taking her gaze off him. Her chest felt like it swelled with all the emotions battling inside her: hope and fear and love.

He stepped inside, into her personal space like he had just under a month ago, when she'd felt like she was taking such a big step letting him into her cabin for the first time. Sitka followed, tail wagging as she pranced next to Sabrina, nudging her leg.

Sabrina couldn't help but smile as she put down her bags and stroked Sitka's fur. She couldn't stop the smile from fading into something more serious as she looked up at Tate, breathed in his familiar sandalwood scent.

"I love you, Sabrina."

Her throat clenched, her own words of love wanting to escape past the barriers she'd put up.

But she'd spent two years being afraid. Two years keeping people at a distance. As much as she wanted it to, that fear didn't just magically disappear simply because the threat of her stalker was gone. The ability to trust again wasn't easy.

Was she keeping Tate at a distance because he'd broken her trust? Or because she'd become afraid to trust her own gut, trust her own feelings?

"I messed up," Tate continued. "And I will forever regret not being more honest with you."

He reached out, took both of her hands in his, and she felt the contact all the way down to her toes.

She had to be honest with herself. In the week

she hadn't seen him, she'd missed this man desperately.

"I know you care about me," he said, his tone as intense as his gaze. "I *know* you do."

She felt herself nodding, saw a brief smile tip the edges of Tate's lips.

Then he was serious again. "We're right together, you and me. If you need more time, I understand and I'll give it to you. But I don't want to wait any longer."

He paused, as if waiting for her to speak, but she couldn't seem to form words before he rushed on.

"I'll do whatever it takes to regain your trust."

She stared up at him, thinking of all the opportunities she'd missed to be with him while she'd lived in Alaska. Thinking of how she'd tried to do what was best for her family, even though it hadn't been what they'd wanted. Of how she'd snuck out in the middle of the night, without a goodbye, so they wouldn't try to follow.

He'd made mistakes, too. But she knew he thought he was protecting her by keeping his past from her. And every time she'd needed him, he'd shown up.

She loved him. She was angry with him, but if she hadn't fallen for him so completely, she wouldn't have been so mad or felt so betrayed.

She couldn't deny what she felt any longer. She didn't want to let her own fear hold her back and lose him. Didn't want to spend the next part of her life missing someone else she loved.

"Whatever you need," Tate repeated, stepping even closer, so she had to tilt her head back to keep staring into his dark, serious gaze. "I know we both need to reconnect with the lives we had to leave. But I want to do it together. I want to see my family again, *finally*, and not feel like I'm compromising their safety or my own by doing it. I want to introduce you to them."

She jerked at the words, at the implied commitment there, and he spoke even faster. "I know you need to go home to your family in New York. I want to meet them. If you want me to," he added. "Whether it's now or later. I want to be with you, whether it's here or in New York or it's long-distance for a while." He glanced at Sitka and added, "The chief has agreed that whatever you want, if you'll let me be with you, Sitka can come, too."

Woof!

He smiled at his dog, then turned his serious gaze back on her. "You can think about this as long as you need. But I won't give up on us. I love you too much, Sabrina."

He let go of one of her hands to cup her cheek. "If you decide you want me to go and leave you alone, I will. But I'll always be waiting. I'll wait as long as it takes."

She stared up at him, words caught in her throat and fear still lodged in her chest.

She loved him. She didn't want to lose him. But was she ready to make such a big leap of faith?

He nodded, gave her a sad smile as he dropped his hand and backed away.

He'd started to turn for the door when she grabbed his arm, gripping tight, knowing it was time to truly move forward. And she couldn't have the life she wanted without him in it.

He turned back, his gaze filled with surprise and a sudden, fierce hope.

"I love you, too, Tate," she croaked, then suppressed a laugh at how tearful she sounded, how joyous she felt. "I love you, too."

Woof! Sitka nudged her again, and Sabrina gave in to the laugh ready to burst inside her. "I love you, too, Sitka."

Then Tate stepped closer, lowered his lips to hers and gently kissed her.

His lips only touched hers for a brief moment, careful of the bruising still coloring her jaw. When he lifted his face again and gave her a huge, brilliant smile, she felt better than she had in more than two years. They'd figure out the details, but she knew one thing for sure: she'd gotten two amazing gifts out of her two years on the run—him and Sitka.

And she wasn't going to ever let them go.

* * * * *

Get 4 FREE REWARDS!

We'll send you 2 FREE Books plus 2 FREE Mystery Gifts.

Harlequin Romantic Suspense books are heart-racing page-turners with unexpected plot twists and irresistible chemistry that will keep you guessing to the very end.

FREE Value Over $20